Joseph Longland

Bernard Alvers and the War Witch

A Poetical Romance in Four Cantos

Joseph Longland

Bernard Alvers and the War Witch
A Poetical Romance in Four Cantos

ISBN/EAN: 9783744772631

Printed in Europe, USA, Canada, Australia, Japan

Cover: Foto ©Andreas Hilbeck / pixelio.de

More available books at **www.hansebooks.com**

AND

The War Witch:

A POETICAL ROMANCE IN FOUR CANTOS.

NEW AND REVISED EDITION;

TO WHICH ARE NOW ADDED

SONGS ON THE LATE WAR WITH RUSSIA.

BY

JOSEPH LONGLAND,

*Author of " Trephely," an Epic Poem, in Five Books; "King Charles the Second,"
an Historical Drama, in Five Acts; "Her Living Shame," a Domestic Drama,
in Three Acts; " The Rose and the Arrow," an Historical Drama, in Three
Acts; " Othello's Incurrence;" and Miscellaneous Poems.*

London:

PROVOST & Co., 36, HENRIETTA STREET, COVENT GARDEN.

1871.

NOTICE.

IT is the intention of the Author to revise and re-issue the whole of his Works; which will be duly announced as they become ready for publication.

PREFACE AND DEDICATION.

THE Romance of "Bernard Alvers and the War Witch" was first published in the year 1850.

Two of the "Songs on the late War with Russia" appeared in a Southampton newspaper at the time of the hostilities. The other "Songs" were written during the Crimean Campaign, but have never appeared in print until now.

The whole of the above have been revised by me during the past year, and are now respectfully dedicated to the public.

JOSEPH LONGLAND.

LONDON, *January*, 1871.

BERNARD ALVERS

AND

THE WAR WITCH.

CANTO I.

" Farewell my home—my home no longer now,
Witness of many a calm and happy day."—Southey.

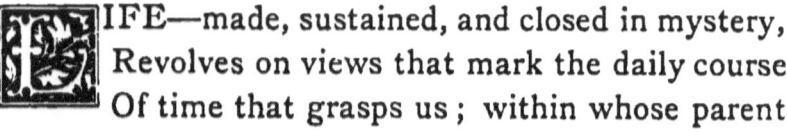

IFE—made, sustained, and closed in mystery,
Revolves on views that mark the daily course
Of time that grasps us ; within whose parent
  range
We fly for breath the moment we are born.
With all our frailties fastened to the hours—
That make the days and years up that convey
The only means of knowing what we know—
We yield, yet hold ; and tremble at the touch
Of that which, if withdrawn, unships us.

Such were the musings of Bernard Alvers as he
wended his way along the country roads of Old
England, in the autumn of the year 1810, intending
to visit his aged parents, in order to take what, in
all probability, would be a final farewell. Bernard
had then served several years in the British Army,
and obtained at last his long-cherished hope—a
furlough; for since he had become a soldier he had
not seen any of his relations. With stick in hand
and knapsack on back, with nature on every side
filling him with a buoyancy that made him feel
thankful for his existence, his reflections were at
first cheerful; but those that more strongly forced
themselves upon him were connected with the circumstance of his present undertaking. He thought
upon his childhood, and the last parting he had with
the friends he was now going to see. He pictured
to himself the joy that would fill the house on his
arrival; but then the fear that this interview might
be the last on earth, gave to his ruminations a
dejected termination. The old couple could not
survive his future absence—no, they were already
silver-grown with age; and he thought that, in the
event of his being ordered to foreign parts, and
doomed to tread the deadly battle-field, though his
life should chance to escape, yet might he return
only to weep over the green swards that would then
cover his parents' ashes.

The travelling soldier became fatigued, for the day
was very hot. At length a running spring beneath a
drooping willow caught his gaze; so he stopped to

drink at the bar of God's public-house, where no charge is asked—no poison vended. Here he refreshed himself with pure water, and sat down within the shade of the willow to rest himself and wipe the sweat from his brow. Being weary, he fell asleep, and dreaming, he fancied himself to be in the same spot where he had sat down, and had merely closed his eyes upon the beauties of the surrounding landscape without losing the view, which was still presented to his mind, but with increased charms. His attention was soon attracted by the appearance in the vision of a being who seemed more than earthly, and who, gliding with the softest ease down the slopes of the distant hills, was evidently making her way towards him. Her feet (for the figure assumed that bewitching sex which makes the human form angelic*) seemed not to touch the earth; not a limb moved, but the whole of the perfect model came onward, sweeping over the tops of the waving corn, and bounding with extreme lightness over every hedge and rivulet that lay in her course, until she arrived at the spot where Bernard reclined. This was the War Witch.

---

* " For spirits when they please,
Can either sex assume, or both ; so soft
And uncompounded is their essence pure;
Not tied or manacled with joint or limb,
Not founded on the brittle strength of bones,
Like cumbrous flesh; but in what shape they choose,
Dilated or condensed, bright or obscure,
Can execute their aëry purposes,
And works of love or enmity fulfil."

Milton's Paradise Lost.

Attired in fabric of a finer web
Than gauze or muslin, yielding to the breeze,
Reflected glosses of the emerald,—
Distinct, but pure,—as if the very dress,
Like her who wore it, were spiritual.
A twisted silver cord of sparkling white
Bound her fair waist and floated far behind,
With ample tassels tipped with burnished gold.
Her hair in auburn tresses laid its length
Below her perfect shoulders, freely flowing
As do the ocean breakers when they curl.
A band of star-lit diamonds crowned her head
And lustred on her forehead's marble hue.
Her eyes were sharper brilliants than the sun,
Glowing in her own firmament of love ;
For love was to her spirit its life's fire,
As spirit is to body made of clay,—
Intenser power and purer, such as heaven's.
Her lips were cloven corals, imported
From the soft rainbow's deep prismatic arch.
Her teeth were pearls, enamelled out of snow
Descending.   Her cheeks were inly tinted
With those inspiring crimson gleams
That manifest *Aurora Borealis.*
Her tiny feet were free, and fair, and bare,
Just as a perfect angel's always are.
So also were her round and graceful arms,
And all her bosom's meek and mighty charms.

This beautiful enchantress stopped her course and closed her journey under the green willow, confronting Bernard dreaming at the spring. He felt, but knew not what; he saw, but could not understand. Charm increased upon charm; sound followed silence. The War Witch spoke, and called him by his name; then all the trees responded in full harmony, and every leaf repeated the melody of her voice. The sky glowed strangely, and the gushing streams burst forth into songs of joy.

She called again, and took him by the hand;
Bernard felt his spirit turn within him.
She told him not to fear—that she had come
His onward course to cheer, and guard him through
The dangerous calling he was 'prenticed to.

Other sons to parents as dear
    As you, may not venture so far;
When the shot and the gleaming spear,
    Shall mark them as victims of war.

To death let them go, for some must
    Feed the glutton as soon as he roars;
Human beings are food for his lust,
    And his feast numbers thousands of scores.

His hoofs are of iron and lead,
    And he prances through oceans of blood;
Behind him he leaves for the dead,
    Peace, pained in a quiet red flood.

Above thy sheltered head the booming guns
Shall bellow forth in vain.   The dripping sword
Shall play its vengeance round thee harmlessly.
Thousands shall fall on thousands down before ;
Their blood shall sprinkle thee—against thy feet
Their slaughtered frames and groaning mouths shall
    meet.

    She warmer pressed his hand,
       And looked him in the face ;
    Too grand to understand
       Was this display of grace.

    It seemed to him that she had made
       Some great mistake of person ;
    Or else some wily trick was played
       On him for some diversion.

    Image of loveliness, I know thee not,
Nor do I know if what I see is real ;
Too much of heaven these moving moments crave
For me of small pretensions to lay claim—
From birth a stranger to felicity.
If I have died I'm saved beyond a doubt,
But if my soul still in my body dwells,
I'm dreaming most deceitful things indeed ;
If thou hast power, wake and undeceive me.

Bernard, witches and spirits are quite real,
Though not corporeal.   You are asleep ;
But though you are, they have permitted power
To link with human spirits' earthly dreams
Some knowledge of their deep concerted schemes,
Made to affect mankind and things below ;
Though but to few such favour do we show.
Yet all the principals who work above,
Have each, on earth, some being that they love,
To whom they do, when they see fit, impart
The tender passion burning in their heart.
And always to some good and useful end
These rare delights and interchanges tend.
No visible weapon in my hand I bear,
To typify the manual work of war.
My mission is one of legislation,
Made special in the cause of Bernard's nation.
There must be management and wise design
In all the deeds of battle.   Grave reasons
Must the grim horrors fairly justify !
I'm first to think and order what shall be,
Then England's heroes work out my decree.

Be not alarmed at what I say,
While you wear this cumbrous clay.
If cruel or reckless I appear
Through war's destructive hot career ;
Remember, all on earth have not
Souls made for heaven's favoured spot,

Or war would never rise.
Hell has its legions mixed below,
In human forms they come and go,
    Like others from the skies;
These for unlawful power aim,
Striving this bright sphere to gain,
    To subjugate its soil;
But stronger heaven averts their will
And guards the favoured planet still—
    Their evil struggles foil.
For this I watch.   To keep hell down
My office is, and saints to crown.

I see the final of the fight
    Before the direful day begins;
I know who'll sleep before that night
    Shall cover with its funeral wings
Eyes that never one more morning
    Shall to conscious joy awaken;
Hearts whose love from those then mourning
    Shall for ever have been taken.

    I breed all thoughts on war,
        And instigate its deeds;
    Urge death's devouring car,
        And smile at widow's weeds.

    I pitch the song of woe,
        And mingle in the wail;

As fast as sorrows flow,
I travel at their tail.
For I'm a merry mischief maker,
And a wholesale undertaker.

Similar offices, in other worlds,
By similar spirits are held; but all
Are carried on in secret, save to those
Who by these privy councillors of state
Have been by love selected for love's sake.
Bernard, fear nothing, you have been my choice;
You cannot make objection—you are mine.
Not now to be in matrimony joined;
For you shall first wear out your human powers
Through all their full and native attributes.
I'm not impatient, though sincere indeed.
Time to me is nothing.   A year to you
Is but a blink of starlight unto me.
Time marks progression in the things of earth,
But holds no *status* in the ways of heaven.
After death, I'll guide your perfect powers
Of spiritual knowledge through galaxies
Of interminable comprehension.

You blood-impassioned clay, with me
Could never right united be;
But I will send you pleasures many,
Of all earth's sons the most of any;
To cheer your heart that long shall know

The force of happiness below.
But when in dying age you swoon,
With every nerve gone out of tune,
I'll wait to greet you at the gate
That opens your immortal state,
And where eternal flowers bloom,
Receive you freshly from the tomb;
To live with me in spacious skies,
And into boundless vision rise.
Then you'll forget what now you hear,
And all the hum of steeds and war;
And all your bygone joys and pains,
Your worldly losses, spoils, and gains,
    Shall never be remembered.
Millions of forms shall there attend,
And at your favoured entrance bend,
Arrayed in light which glory gives,
Where only what is holy lives;
To you they all shall speak in praise,
While round you brighter light shall blaze,
    In richer hues than theirs.
And then 't shall be your lot to see
The wonders of eternity.
Not to gaze, as mortals do
On earth, at wondrous things they view,
Yet fail to grasp the fading glare
Which dazzles to deceive them there.

The mighty vast which heaven reveals,
 Makes joy without a sigh;
The sense that sees in heaven, feels
 Stupendous floods rush by.

Established hope throws off the veil
 It whispered through below;
And swelling into vocal throngs,
The music of immortal songs
 Commence their endless flow.

Live on, till that consummate time,
Where war's applauded laurels shine,
 And valour wins a prize.
Where praise is rare, but freely given,
To gallant greatness under heaven,
 By statesmen great and wise.
And let your loudest words on earth
Be about your country's worth—
 Her proud heroic deeds.
I'll join your patriotic song,
And help the harmony along;
I'll dwell upon your lips and smile—
Your leisure moment all beguile
 With thoughts that flow with ease;
And every time you want a line,
The diction of it shall be mine,
 As often as you please.
You've many a subject in your way,

And many a curious thing to say;
You'll wonder sometimes how they grow
Spontaneously before your view,
Unasked for and untaught, to rise
In groups of life before your eyes,
Flashes of joy to make you feel
There's something in your spirit, real
    And unexplained below.   ·
Farewell!   I'll make you my chief care,
I'll shield you round in peace and war,
    Wherever you may go.

The War Witch closed her maiden speech,
    She waved her lily hand;
And Bernard's straining eyes grew dim—
    The Witch invisible.

Bernard awoke, and life with its stern realities
returned.   A change of feeling had worked upon him,
and like thousands who at times awake from pleasing
dreams, he felt himself deceived.   Still, he could not
divest his mind from the impression that he was
under the influence of some spiritual agent, and,
striving to banish the gloom of disappointment, he
exclaimed—

This world is a merry round rolling ball,
    And I am a merry young gay man;
'Tis misery to want what we don't at all,
    And wise to drive sorrow away, man.

The sky with its blue contributes to me
  As much as it does to a king's lungs;
My eyes as much of broad nature can see,
  And fancy assume richer kingdoms.

No longer then I'll endure my life,
  But longer essay to enjoy it;
And O while it makes me feel so blithe,
  Why should I in folly annoy it?

But hush! another sound is heard!
    And Bernard stops!
'Tis not from man, nor beast, nor bird,
    The music drops!
Yet something in the air steals by
On wings of sumptuous melody;
And words of beauty, all on fire,
Fly forth from this mysterious lyre!

    And you my love shall be;
My constant love, my only love,
    For you were born for me.
Make haste above, immortal dove,
    Where you my joys shall see.

My soul is indeed linked in with spirits of most
absolute existence, and the charmed atmosphere
conveys to my ears their inhuman freaks. Is man
entirely passive—a mere piece of mechanism—the

B

subject of others' wills, before life and after it ;—
forced onward through changes that destinate an
order of things of which he knows nothing—not
even himself?   O, then, I am pitiably portioned with
a little knowledge and the want of more!   Better for
me I had been born some little bird, to fly without
disturbing thoughts through a short triumphant day,
kissing the sky as if it were my own, and leaving
every spot I loved not, to try the taste of changes
every hour.

I'm on the tree
Of transient glee,
Where I'm sure I shall not always be ;
Striving to breathe, and feel, and see,
On life's great tree.

The winds rush past
The leaves so fast,
I roll like waves upon the sea ;
While branches wave
Above the grave,
That ever threatens life's great tree.

New mornings break,
Thousands awake,
And yawn upon the moving tree.
Ere night comes round,
Low under ground
Lie thousands of leaves from life's great tree.

Bernard at length arrived at the spot of his early affection. Unable to shake off impressions that had engaged his mind with such uncommon thoughts, he passed many things in his journey unnoticed, which otherwise would have afforded him subjects for pleasant reflection. But Bernard was an altered man, though not so much affected in a strange way as to be indifferent to the scenery that burst upon his view, as he entered the village where all his child-dreams had been created and enjoyed.

He changed again ! The Parish Church was there,
And graves whose history he so well knew ;
The very stile he often sat upon
Still led the way to that sage edifice
Whose walls enclosed him when he first received
The name of Bernard. Pensively it stood,
Waiting by Time's own sleepless hands to fall,
And perish in forgetfulness.

A little further on he perceived his long-lost home. His heart bounded to the spot, and he was soon amongst his kindred, reciprocating the smiles and happy greetings of those whose affections his own belonged to. Here he felt rushing into his soul the long ebbed tide of early love, which, for a few times in life, is suffered to return, and then rolls away for ever !

Where in this vain and pompous world exists
Unsullied love as nature makes it—pure ?

Unscathed by fashion and the pride of rank,
And also free from demonstrations wild?
Where no deceptive treasure gleams to lure;
No lordly manor courts the high-born heir;
No fostered offices of state congeal
Truth's bright humility; no unwise neglect
Leaves fav'rite sons to roam the world unchecked?
The meekest home that claims the mountain side,
With spacious air and heaven spread above,
In whose secluded nook Affection guides
In simplest form of words the counsel taught,
And chastely governs the contented hearts
That she thus trains;—there likeliest is love.

Bernard retired to rest that night far from the
noisy barrack-room, relieved from the din of arms
and every sound that tells of military life. He was
again a cherished member of civil society, and peace-
fully lodged in the bosom of his native circle. A few
months more, and where shall we then find him?

Softly as evening breezes die,
    Fainting beneath the stars,
The War Witch at his bed stole by,
    And hushed his mortal cares.

She laid her angel form upon
    The pillow where he breathed,
And stretched her downy wings across
    The body she relieved.

And every respiration thrown
From out his tired clay,
She caught as life that was her own,
And purged his sighs away.

Light gently beamed—a holy, mellow glow,
Where mortal and immortal lay entwined,
Tinted the darkness.   All there was dead—
At least seemed dead—save what was spiritual.
Bernard, entranced, beheld a group approach,
Attended by the lovely Witch he knew,
Whose power produced the vision in the dream.
His parents, decked with righteousness and smiles,
Devoutly looking upwards into heaven,
Came on ; and in the train came following
His brothers and his sisters with like grace—
All dignified with special happiness—
Singing to God praises for their creation.
O how choice it then appeared to him,
How highly favoured to have been ordained
A member in that holy family!

The War Witch smiled upon her spell-bound choice,
And said : These are thy honoured friends, and this
Thy envied home.   Prime earth hath brought thee
    forth,
Yielded thee life, and in thy fashioned frame
Enclosed the heart that mine's affianced to.
Early I watched thee when, within her arms

Whom rev'rence calls thy mother, life held thee
In its tenderest innocence.
Over thy infant cradle I was there,
Hoping for thee and me, and chiding off
Assailing efforts made by spirits dark,
And others of celestial heritage,
Who came in hosts to battle for thy soul;
For, at its birth, high up, through heaven's vault,
Sounding loud and echoing to and fro,
Past hell, and further on, came news of thee.
All stirred amazed! Heaven's arch rose higher up—
The zenith yawned, and thundered forth a voice,
Then closed the blackened void, and back again,
Below its native level, fell the pall!
Swelling with force came clouds of ghastliness,
Terrific to the angels! Confusion
Followed the disturbance, and unripe wonder
Grew pallid on the astonished multitude!
A momentary silence then prevailed,
And hushed were our celestial praises.
Hell with its clanging arms made motion first
To sally forth. Heaven listened as these fiends,
Making for earth, roared shouts of savage glee;
Then, heaving off its pent-up breath in haste,
Summoned aloud its glittering garrison.
Clans mustered into close concerted throngs
On groups of clouds, declaiming zealously;
Each host divine its special conference held,
Arrayed alike for instantaneous war.

Then boldly with my myriads I rushed in—
Declared to all the assembled forces there
My ancient war prerogative, and sued
For just preferment.   Jealous of my haste
My rivals copied my example; all
Claimed rights equal, and permission begged
To rescue earth's new gem.

                  Consent was given,
And down in vulture swiftness gaily rushed
Th' excited cherubim!   A storm of spirits,
Raised into a tempest, shook the round vault!
The universe, alarmed, unhinged its laws;
Stars stopped their twinkling; and every planet
Moved aside to let fierce heaven pass!
This poor earth trembled as it never did
Since its first circle round the sun was made;
For since that day, which man can never date,
It never had been so assailed from hell—
It never had been so assailed from heaven.
The greatest powers of everlasting life
Aimed at its sides in one compound assault
Enough to rend it into dust; their force,
Their angry breath, that dust would blow away.

But stronger ardour burns in angels' hearts,
For love of love, than doth in demons' wills;
So, loving more, we made the greater speed,
Gained more in time than those from hell set out,

And overtook the savage pack before
They smelt the verge of earth's thin atmosphere;
There we challenged them, and then we charged!
Their ranks confused, we kept confusion up,
Disjointed all their order, drove them back,
And scattered o'er the stretch of emptiness
Their undone strength.   Away on every side
They rushed, yelling the notes of darkness damned,
Sore beaten—disappointed—agonized!

   The fray thus closed, I faced again to earth,
Redressed my champions, whose triumphant glee
Sounded like rejoicing thunder.   Once more
Our prosperous journey we dashed forth upon;
For rivals of our own class followed hard
Upon us; we heard their flapping wings
Cleave space with breathless force!
So closely on us in their speed they bore
That all their struggles echoed through our own.

   The various worlds we compassed in our course
Had life revived in all their buried dead,
Who came, with all the quick, to look at us
And spectator our terrific onslaught.
Mute wonder then cramped all phenomena;
Order took fright, and far into the bowels
Of every stagnant globe shrunk dormant
Gravitation!   Ethereal splendour,
In dishevelled gait, blanched into distance

Paralyzed! Heedless I passed the panic spheres,
Nerved like a giant with his hot blood up,—
No cold delay relaxed our combined eagerness.
Our great display, our haste, our shouts of joy,
At length began to tell upon the world;
Suddenly it stood, like other worlds, confused!
Then from its aqueous magazines gushed forth
Clouds of suffocating vapour!—dark, dense,
And dismal as the depths of Erebus!
Into this appalling wilderness we charged,
Through nauseous darkness pushed our willing way.
But while we thus hot-blanketed in death
To all invisible, though still in fierce pursuit,
Loud in their deep convulsive struggles burst
"The war of elements." Both in their best,
The lightning and the thunder ruled supreme—
Shot flames, and tore the troubled air about
In waves and gaps of fierce displacement wild!
Converging then, anon, dense lobes of cloud,
Compressed together for more horrid work,
Again with rapid rents and roars went off,
Till every orbit in the universe gave out,
And dislocated the entire creation!

This was the time for me to cheer my troops;
I rushed in front—stood on a compact mass
Of unexploded cloud—besought my God—
And thus addressed my panting legions brave:
Gems of the Palace Royal, to me give ear;

Beyond this mist of matter's jealousy
Lies the object of our venturous exploit,
Cradling in innocence, and beautiful as rare.
Another plunge, and on his quiet slumbers
We shall alight, and for awhile repose.
Endure the awe we are now immerged in,
United with whose smoke competing seraphs
Have not yet come in—now, cannot pass us.
The time for conquest is becoming ripe—
Our firmness soon shall bring us victory.
All the listening universe looks down upon
Our deeds, has watched us into this eclipse,
And waits to view us disengage ourselves
Beneath, and breast the lower air.

    While I spoke the thunder's rolls receded;
The changing clouds grew bright, and so did we.
I beckoned, turned, and made a final charge,
Cleared out from gloom, and through the blissful blue
Of clear transparent atmosphere, sailed on
Triumphantly !
The placid earth, changed from its useless wrath,
Received our front with smiles.   'Twas morning,
And the peaceful sea rolled softly to the shore,
The verdant fields sustained a pleasant dew,
The feathery tribe sang new-born-day in gladness ;
The villages with early drifting smoke
Fretted the homely sphere with tokens of
Humanity; while scattered mountain streams

Told gentle tales of Nature's undulations.
Thus played the fickle world its harmony
When I approached with all my train thy home,
When I alighted with my heavenly host,
Where thy dear mother sang thy lullaby;
I claimed thee then from her, and with a mark—
Which eyes of clay are wanted not to see—
I stamped a token which thy forehead bears.
Perched high above the cloud-cleared wilderness,
Our outstripped rival brethren gazing stood,
Wondering at my clean accomplishment.
More shall be told to thee of all these things
In after life, when thy unprisoned soul
Is purified, and all its freedom free.

———————

The hours of the night stole over the dwelling of
the soldier with uninterrupted stillness. The passing traveller, and nocturnal tribe—few and unnatural
to man—that search the darkness for existence, saw
nothing unusual, nor heard a wakeful sound break
round that quiet cabin. The house-dog's slumbers
were unmolested, the wicket-gate remained unstirred,
and every inmate slept on at ease.

Bernard arose the next morning almost with the
sun. The prime of youth blushed fresh upon his
cheeks. The tales of many years were not yet
engraved upon his features; but in his father's

countenance he saw Time's inevitable intrusions,
which, though they made him sigh, made him love
the more.

What is it, father, that has dimmed thine eyes,
Which once were clear and bright and full of life,
In which I saw thy living soul see me ?
Recedes the spirit backward in the flesh,
More inward to its native seat, the heart ?
Or does it from thy frame evaporate,
Disliking thy infirmity ?
Thy feeble lips the question cannot solve ;
The vivid flame ebbs on their failing strength
Reviveless.   O my father !—yet my father !—
Is what is gone of thee gone for ever ?

Who shall compress those lips of honoured mould,
    When death shall change their wonted crimson
        hue ?
What living child of thine shalt thou behold
    To whisper in his ears thy last adieu,
When on the verge of this life's painful flood
Thy passing soul steps forth to meet its God ?

Who shall be here to catch the meaning stare,
    The latest glance of those concluding eyes ?
To close their darkened orbs, and to prepare
    The solemn rites of funeral obsequies ?
If I'm not here, my heart shall swell the more,
If such news finds me on a foreign shore.

Son, the world itself is advancing into age like the body of your time-worn parent; and the mighty sun which now opens his face upon us, will yet have to close his great light and shut up his countenance for ages, perhaps for evermore! Should this make him shine in sorrow? Such would be useless, for it could not alter his destiny. How brightly he enjoys his fading existence! Let us imitate him. The golden morning of returning spring, that streaks the vault of heaven with richer tints than absent fancy can.command, sports joyfully its short-lived glory over the fields, until it yields its existence to the influence of approaching noon. Let us imitate the joyful morning. The tender velvet flowers that decorate the luxuriant earth, giving odour to the breath of heaven and proclaiming the excellence of their Maker's taste, blush annually with unaltered hues, as fresh and as gay as when they first greeted our original parents in Paradise. Let us, like the flowers, exhibit no grief for our inevitable destiny; and like the happy birds of the air, who never dream of death, sing merrily over a well-spent life, from morning until evening, and drown its useless mopings in cheerful and innocent recreations. This is what philosophy inculcates, and wisdom adopts. Strange, that everything we see appears more philosophical and wiser than man!

Bernard's sojourn in his native place being profitably and affectionately disposed of, the time arrived for him to rejoin his regiment, and he had to say the painful "farewell"—that last and searching word,

which acts as a lever to the heart, and holds its
power unaltered through all the changes of time.

   Come, father, mother, and sisters—all come
With me to yon graveyard ; there let us part,
Where we may yet all meet, to mingle on,
Through long forgetfulness, our dust and bones.
Come cheerfully ! The place is sad, yet come,
For at this time a fitting place it is
For us to separate. In my road it lies,
And there, above the low yew-shaded graves,
At which we've often sighed and wept before,
Let us in union drop our parting tears.
There our two other sisters lie, and there
I'll part from all with one affection—
The living and the dead together.

   They all approached the spot—they all would speak,
But grief prevented them ; and the same words
Each felt might cheer the other, felt they all ;
For every case was special, every tongue
Alike, and sorrow all the same. Then who
Shall speak the first ? The good old man,
The father, changed the sobbing into words—
Embraced them all, and bade his son
Command his tears and put on manliness.

   Father, I'm too much a man ; yet for love
I'll yield to one so kind. Too much like God !

Too sensible! yet for thy sake I'll thank Him
For my being, with which He honours me
Through thee. Had I in dull creation's scale
Instinctive only been, to fly, or crawl,
Or swim, much less I should have felt,
Much less have mourned, much less enjoyed.
Then if more pain insures to me more love,
Again I thank my God submissively.
Death soon shall all the circumstances close
That fret our peevish clay; then for ever
Dies the sting—for ever lives the love.
How blessed then to feel that we shall all
In God be lost, and in that loss be saved!

Bernard, when you're far removed
From us that you have so much loved,
And tempting evils press you round,
On native or on foreign ground,
        Remember this sad scene.
Where vice, with all its wily smiles,
Incautious, easy man beguiles;
Where busy fraud and gaming lore
Engage the thoughts of minds impure;
Where converse with immoral aim,
And songs of low immoral strain,
Unite to wake your evil will;—
Remain our Bernard Alvers still,
        As true as you have been.
For those who share the greater trials,

And suffer harder self-denials,
　　Shall greater conquerors prove.
And should we ne'er again on earth
Unite to share our woes and mirth,
　　We'll mingle joy above.
And may thy heart, which long was ours, ·
That cheered us in our playful hours,
　　Ne'er break with sorrow down.
May the storms that shall surround thee
Never raise a flood to drown thee;
But in thine ear the ocean's roar
Seem like an echo from the shore
Of wishes meant to cheer thee on,
And joy to hail thy coming home,
　　From us, when thou art gone.

　　These were the words of Bernard's affectionate
sisters.　They could proceed no further, for their
souls began to flow over as they joined in the last
sentence.　Bernard now began in earnest to put on
manliness, for he saw that lamentation was becoming
too afflicting and pressing too heavily upon the feelings of his overwrought parents.

　　Kind are these tears, but, sisters weep no more,
Let misery die, and grief depart this life;
Glory has set its seal upon my brow,
And with a golden finger beckons me
To go.　A whisper bids me follow it,

Though thorns and briars bestrew the flinty path;
It tells me fortune and renown are there,
But not at home.   O it would never do
For growing sons, with man's rough nature clad,
To waste or misapply their youthfulness.
The broad world calls them, and they must away,
To serve their end, and duty's calls obey.

Fame must be sought for—glory be fought for,
    Death of itself will come.
Whate'er it may yield I'm off to the field;
For England alone my weapons I'll wield,
    Bayonet, or sword, or gun.
For none would I fight but the bold and free—
Britannia and right, dominion and sea;
The steadfast of nations, thank God it is mine;
The birthplace of heroes—this island divine!

END OF CANTO I.

C

CANTO II.

"My choir shall be the moonlit waves,
   When murm'ring homeward to their caves;
   Or when the stillness of the sea,
   E'en more than music breathes of thee."—*Moore.*

THE bugle calls—through barrack walls
   Resound its loud alarms!
Soldiers, to-day no show nor play
   Demands your ready arms.

Raise up your heads from iron beds,
   Ye sons of Mars, arise;
No victory comes to silent drums,
   Nor dull and drowsy eyes.

Dream, dream no more of peace on shore,
   The battle-day is nigh!
Go forth and show our haughty foe
   How bravely Britons die.

Bernard was not the last out of bed on that excitable morning. It seemed as if the sun, as he rose his majestic head above the horizon, had sounded forth the alarm; for all was bustle and stir, not only in the faithful garrison but also in the adjoining town, the inhabitants of which were all on tip-toe, talking of invasions, foreign yokes, slaughtered relations, and Buonaparte's ostensible ascendency over Great Britain and the world. They consequently felt a lively interest in watching the movements of the troops preparing to embark for the Spanish peninsula.

Again the bugle sounds—they muster;
Falling in, they rank by rank count souls,
    Skilled in the field's manœuvres.
Many a heart that's there shall bleed,
    And in its dying gore
    Exult for England's glory!

What, after all, is human wreck,
If out of that necessity
    Comes victory?
What crushing joints, and shouts,
And gasps that let in death,
If conquest crowns the rush
Made mighty through the ranks
    Of enemies?

Mute, obedient, firm as the pyramids
They stand; clothed outward with rude instruments,
But inward with real strength. The blood they hold
Is England's wealthiest ore—the richest

Of her riches! With this she purchases
Kingdoms and thrones and territorial sway,
Which nothing else could buy. It's a forced coin,
And when once offered works its way itself.

The town is all in motion! The soldiers are
marching off, and the diverting band has opened
its brazen voice to the tune of "The British Grena-
diers." Handkerchiefs are waved from windows,
and many cheers, with prayers and tears, salute
each passing regiment. The time being short, and
orders peremptory, the soldiers soon found themselves
under sail, and making progress across the deep
waters.

Stupendous and absorbing ocean flood!
Whose throbbing bosom spaciousness reveals,
And awes the mind with earth's great glory spread!
O what relief the dusty landsman feels
When shipped upon thy wilderness:
No street-cries' trafficking, no brewers' drays,
No herds, no funeral throngs pass here;
Here the coarse hum of busy life is hushed,
And all that dares to breathe is heaven;
Here the broad day rejoices in its light,
While waves harmonious sing disturbless songs
In praise of Deity. Calm or enraged,
They solo and they chorus Him who made them;
Then burnish up a mirror to display

Reflections of the million stars aloft,
And the bright line the moon makes round the world.

    Night steeps itself in sleep,
      And cooling breezes fly
    Across the sombre deep,
      Beneath a twinkling sky.

    The bugle's last post sounds,
      And echoes far at sea;
    The night-watch goes its rounds;
      The careful ship sails free.

    Swung between decks, where hundreds more are swung, slumbers Bernard Alvers. Should he escape the dangers of the sea, the cannon's mouth stands ready upon the shore to blaze upon him. Alas! and is it not enough that life, with its fatal accidents,—disease, with its preventless bolts,—age, with its inevitable blast, should make assailment on men's frail systems, to sweep their pleasures to the tomb; but that artificial wreck, wholesale breakage, scientific devastations, should be used to aid dull nature's sloth, and drive remorseless horrors through mankind! O why is love so weak that passion masters it?

    Beyond the sight of land she steers,
      Where deeper waters keep
    The buoyant shipload's unroused fears
      In unmolested sleep.

Around her sides the dolphins play,
Where slipp'ry moonbeams dance;
Like meteors rushing fast away,
That quite as fast advance.

Who is he that dreams, that slumbers in peace profounder than kings are favoured with, that breathes celestial air refined with spirits' spells; and holds communion with immortal messengers?

It is Bernard that dreams,
And the War Witch that means
To assail him again;
But unknown to the men
Who sleep close by his side,
Borne along on the tide;
There's nothing can balk her
On land or on water;
So she's out for a spree
On the plains of the sea,
And to fully employ
A few hours in joy,
She has garnished the night
With everything bright.

She has locked up the winds of heaven in the caves of the rocky shores, ordered below all the monsters that flounder on the top of the main, swept clean away all clouds that hung like cobwebs in the

sky, and made the whole of nature beautiful to cheer
the soul of him she seeks to entertain.   All safe
without, within the ship she reigns.

How deep is the ocean here ?
A thousand fathoms down,
Where we in our curbless cheer
   Sing lays to the ocean crown ;
Sing, till we are tired of glee,
   To Neptune and his crew ;
And sing till we drain the sea
   Of all its dripping blue.

These words, which Bernard listened to with
breathless attention, seemed to issue from the bed
of the ocean, on whose surface he found himself
(reclining upon some substance which floated upon
that great desert), beneath the most brilliant sky he
had ever beheld.   The sounds ceased, and his ears
being disengaged, he made exclusive use of his eyes,
and gazed upon the stretch of distance displayed
upon that naked hemisphere.   Never before had the
world appeared to him so grand.   Never before had
he beheld such uncovered extension.   But what a
mite it made of himself—what a piece of nothing
upon that interminable magnificence !   There lay
the inexplicable creation around him, glowing with
mute speech, performing the meaning of every silent
word, and venting rapture in the harmony of its
existence.

" We'll skim o'er the sea,
In our native glee,"
Sang thousands under the water.
" The Monarch is coming to look at the sky,
To view the round moon with his cold briny eye,"
Sang thousands under the water.

A clattering stir of things alive
Made Bernard's wondering spirit strive
To understand, by earnest gazing,
What the real dust was they were raising.
Up, up, they came, and down they went,
For all seemed on diversion bent.
At length, the discord getting hushed,
They into mutual order rushed ;
In beauty's form, with mermaid's grace,
Each spirit took a special place,
Then quite at home, danced round in glee,
Like things that scarcely touched the sea,
And sang the following theme :

" Now up and down we'll drive a song,
As merry as the night is long ;
Over, about, throughout, upon,
These silvery shining billows.

" The moon we love,
The stars we love,
And our beautiful selves we dearly love ;

The night's our day,
Long may it stay,
With our banqueting on this liquid way."

The sea becomes transparent; at its base
Bernard perceives, distinctly as they are,
All rough and raw, things hid for ever there!
Rocks, weed-beds, boulders huge, caverns, and crags
Immense! Ravines deep with terror,
And coral-reefs studding the labyrinth!
Throughout this dim confusion horrible,
Behold, light coruscates the scenery!
And fitful as it gleams those notes revive
Of that strange melody that just declined;
Anon they faint, and then anon grow fierce,
And roll about like living tongues that love
To cling upon the moisture of the waves.

While the eye winks the active ocean heaves,
Coils up its yielding fluid, and retreats
In glassy mountains, modelled and upheld!
As suddenly a smooth soft vale sinks deep,
And beautifies the concave thus dipped out.
This vast arena soon develops life,
And climbing up the lofty avalanches,
Are seen those charming Naiades, who sang
Just now below the pliant element.
Perched on every glistening top sits one,
Invested with a harp whose strings are fire.

A shout—they sing, they boldly strike,
 They tune those harps of joy;
And all these blessed saints invite
 King Neptune to pass by.

And lo! responses deep are sung
 Beneath the valley's base;
Then, mingling, all unite in one,
 To rend the living place.

The passive waters vibrate to the praise
Thus offered to their undiscovered king;
While, issuing forth from all the sloping sides
Of this huge hollow's grand circumference,
Fresh millions of the spirit tribe appear,
Who rise, descend, and cross each other round
With all the ease that clouds obey the wind.
Not fallen beings are they—never were,
Nor mortal either, made alive to die;
But bred in the bosom of offenceless waves,
And born relations to all sinless forms,
With shapes as pliant as their fancies are,
To suit their social and peculiar joys.

Besides all these another train comes up;
Now seen beneath the centre of the deep.
All eyes are turned below, all harps are raised,
And round this burnished empire chorus rings!
Amidst this drowning unity of sound—

Whose efforts thrill to sweet intoxication,
And into death drive nature's other works—
Rises great Neptune and his councillors!

His beard is weeds in matted curls,
His robe is fringed with foam,
His jewels are the purest pearls
Discovered in his home.

Seated upon a rugged rock—his throne,
Unchiselled native of the purling main;
He rises slowly like a Prince supreme,
With ancient prestige stamped upon his looks.
With agates, and spars, and diamonds rare,
Profusely he emerges, and profusely
He is viewed.　His trident arm is raised,
And all the lyres are hushed, silent as chaos.
His glances run that towering concave round,
Measuring their own dignity.　On him,
In loyal love, the eyes so numberless
Of all these beaming Thetises look down,
Which seem a fixed continuance of stars
That twinkle overhead; spangling alike
Above, below, one rich unbroken universe.

Subjects and ministers of my empire!
The homage paid me in this marvellous scene
I do accept, and mingle joy with joy.

Now, with your wonted readiness, obey
My voice, and blend this night and melody
Together in one concurrent harmony.
And when the dawn of obvious day begins
To creep along the wakeful eastern ridge,
We'll pull our unexhausted pleasures down,
And revel in the bowels of the sea.
These lofty liquid walls, at once drop down,
Disperse these hills to ocean's furthest verge,
And make again our aqueous carpet smooth.
Then spread yourselves about upon the plain,
Ye forms that charm the weakness of a king,
And tune to me your songs of loyal love,
While I recline, full length, to listen to
Your blissful bars, and court the placid moon.

Down fell the crystal battlements anon!
Destroyed was then that amphitheatre.
The sudden sinking of the dispelled weight,
Submerging to its wonted level rest,
Upset the yielding fluid all around,
Till on the far horizon it was seen
Breaking its force, and fringing our huge world
In one great ring of disconcerted froth!
The harpers, on all sides diverging, spread,
Enjoying their obedience. But the bliss
They feel who know how to distribute it,
Is not the tenth part of the happiness
Enjoyed by him and those who ravish it.

Neptune disposes, as he said, his length,
Supported on the waters' salty strength,
Smiling upon the moon's consoling face,
Which lights his throne and gives him grace for grace.
He unto her a perfect mirror lends,
And she to him a full acceptance sends.

The sea belongs to one great king,
  And round the world he rides;
His honours, in the storms we sing,
  His triumphs, in the tides.

There's grandeur in his fervent race,
  Compassion in his eye;
His tender bosom finds a place
  For thousands doomed to die.

His arm's the strongest arm on earth,
  His hand the softest hand;
He reigns despotic from his birth,
  And terrifies the land.

Something destroys the humid god's repose!
A hideous frown creeps on his bending brows,
And wrath flies forth from his indignant eyes!
Heedless of lavished honours he gets up—
Draws his stretched limbs together eagerly—
Commanding all his harpers to come in.

The moving of this multitude gives birth
To troubled air, before, so soft and still,
That waves beneath their agitation rise,
Changing the quiet scene to tumult.

Saints of my disputeless empire—Behold !
Saw you a rival as you passed along ?
Saw you a mortal slave reclined, where I
Hold single majesty ?—Mocking my power,
Tempting himself with my divinity,
Swinging his body on my exclusive home,
And trifling with my sole prerogative ?
Saw you the miscreant, stretched and at ease,
Now tossing and panting with a landsman's fear
Upon those tiny hillocks you have caused
By being so obedient ?   Again clear off—
Stand all aside—and see how soon that speck
Shall sink to rise no more.

Imperious serf, bold withering worm,
Thou mote of daintless spawn—I charge you, speak,
And tell me how you came upon my wilds,
Where nothing human is acknowledged free ?
O ! for this presumptuous trespassing,
For this rude mocking of my mightiness,
I'll work upon your inward power that thinks,
For there the greatest agony finds birth,
And there it is my privilege to inflict
Aches and throes of such fierce chastisement,

That the rebuke shall heave its anguish back
Through fifty generations gone before
Of thy despised and filthy dying race !
What ! have you ever seen the great sea yawn
Down to its deepest den, where lowest lies
The leaden fluid cold, beneath whose weight
Are sights and secrets unexplored by man ?
And have you ever heard in your short life
The overbalanced earth crack at the gulf
So stretched ?
I have such ghastly corners down below—
Such holes—such frightful living things that move,
That, once beheld by thee, would quickly drive
Thy puny understanding into madness !
I'll give you one example of this truth,
For I detest the feeling in your blood
That made you thus presume.
Waters, obey my voice, and round about
This floating foreigner, depart !   Leave him
Perched in a void, through which he straight shall fall
Into the glooms that ye shall now unfill.

The sea moves not, though its own king commands !
But, calming down, keeps dazzling to the moon.
At such grave disobedience, the vexed king
Grows into boundless fury, and rears up
In bitter indignation his hot head,
As if to draw, by threatening mien, a curse
Upon the large disloyal flood !

But suddenly his rigid limbs collapse,
And under some sharp mental stroke received,
This god's rash threat recoils upon himself!
Still he holds courage in reserve; for lo!
His heart revives—again he feels his place,
But not his power. He tries the waves again;
Again they disobey, while Bernard floats,
Unmoved in spirit, undisturbed in limb.
Neptune, confused, throws out his tattered weeds,
Swells into stronger rage, drops on his throne,
And flounders where he stood. Seething in brine,
The fallen god deplores this mutiny.
His loves in sad dejection dive below,
To hide their grief where tears can never flow.
Again he lifts his mortified crowned head
To see if Bernard still is trespassing;—
This culprit, Bernard, then but smiles; when lo!
Fresh-lit vengeance brings the god right up,
Reanimated with his last despairing plunge;
He looks and calls for aid to heaven above,
Or empire in some more obedient world.

Now the shocked moon begins to swell herself,
Dilating o'er one half the concave heavens.
The stars, subdued by her increasing light,
Faint out of view. The troubled sea rolls high,
And spoils the late appearance of the scene.
Bang goes the moon, exploded like a shell
That heaven hurled forth with grand majestic force!

D

The noise out-terribles the dire event.
Rent into fragments, the fiery spars
Encumber space, and trespass downwards
In our atmosphere.

           Neptune, rebuked,
Low with his coward head lies down—quite low;
Paralyzed where lately he was praised.
His ears in anguish listen to a voice
That speaks from every flying remnant
Of the ruined moon—" Touch not God's anointed."
Sinking in the sea, the burning splinters
Grumble through the flood, and under Neptune's
Tottering throne revel enraged!

   Black grows the sky at its absent glory;
Red grow the stars all twinkling in fury;
Red grows the sea beneath their reflection;
Thick grows the air disturbed by contention!
Now on the horizon's dim distant verge
There rises a swelling and rolling surge;
It froths and it whitens, and gets brighter,
And the great waste of waters grows lighter;
And far on its green banks spirits are seen,
In clusters surrounding some Naiades' queen,
Moving here, moving there, and making their way,
All the time, every turn, to where Bernard lay.
There's one in the centre of that gay throng,
Seems anxiously driving the rest along;

For she has something to do, something to say,
And all to get over before break of day.
The watery nymphs below, now and then
Peep up and pop down under water again;
Splashing and dashing in curious glee,
Just glancing to catch what there is to see;
But afraid to come up on the changed expanse,
Now a new caste of spirits usurp the dance;
Yet anxious to know what's afloat to be done,
And why they were stopped of their native fun,
And what strange fish it was Neptune saw,
That filled the king's spirit and heaven with awe,
And split up the moon and darkened the sky,
And sent a new flock of gay revellers by.

Let passion never stir a god;
    In it dwells no virtue.
Despair not, Neptune, at my rod;
I'll use it, being a higher god,
    But do not mean to hurt you.

I am the War Witch, made by heaven
    To rule men's fate down here.
Your godship is to keep the main;
Fishes *et cætera* you can claim,
Command and rule, or praise or blame,
    But not a human creature.

The " serf," the " miscreant," " withering worm,"
That you so ignominously abused,

Is more to me than you are to these depths!
To your dull eye he may appear a "mote,"
But in my keen glance he fills a space
Equal to heaven and earth.
Are you a king?   And saw you not his mark
Glowing with bright distinctness on his brow?
This was his passport to your drenching realms—
Through God's dominions everywhere he's free.

Come, Bernard, come here to your War Witch love,
And witness a sketch of my power above.
Come forward, and show to this vanity king,
What genuine pleasures my darling can bring;
What a store of love, what banqueting fair,
Your soul can emit and your lips can share.
Come show him your form and softness of heart,
    And make him repent of his words,
In telling the terrible waters to part,
    And turn your thin blood into curds.

The War Witch waves her hand, and all her hosts
In order and in bright array stand forth;
Increasing fast from heaven, down they come,
And congregate around her on the sea.
Nearing this assembly, Bernard is hailed
With shouts acclamatory that travel down
All earth's declining sides.
Oh, how much richer were these sounds than those
That Neptune gloried at!   Though chastely strung

And eloquently taught, his melodists
Learnt not among the skies their native notes !
Their songs were born among the droning waves,
Whose frothy tops for ever curl and heave
To one monotony.   But these brave souls,
Who sing him into strange astonishment,
Were taught their chiming in another school ;
'Mong twinkling stars they learnt to vary sounds,
And all that's bright and spangled in the heavens
Are notes to them of music.

The War Witch now, with rapid bursts of joy,
Takes Bernard's hand and looks him in the face.
She makes no effort to conceal that joy,
Which she knows well the lad reciprocates.
Then, to show her willingness to serve him—
To make her own joy greater by the deed,
And grant him some indulgence on his way,
Invites him to demand of her some favour.

Kind giver of felicity, not now;
I could not now invent another wish ;
Such avarice my full heart banishes.
This scene makes void desire, and loads my soul
With love's entire and sealed accomplishment.
Here at thy feet for ever let me dwell,
And let this full eternity go on
Blazing upon me in its evermore.
Stop not this ' kingdom come '—so well begun.

O ! let no period again step in.
This is my wish—that changelessness may be :
Not for any act to be performed,
Not for anything now to be supplied,
But for suspension and continuance.
But if I only dream, but falsely dream,
Which all my joys have hitherto but been ;
And still if thou hast power, still grant me aid,
For I should then a favour really want,
Which is, to keep me in this dreaming state—
To guard my body that it may not wake—
To let me never on the ills of life
Emerge again, where all is pain and strife.
I've now seen both, and this is my desire—
To finish where I am, and thus retire.

The earth recedes with all that it contains
Save Bernard and the Witch, who float in air.
The ocean king, left in the boiling brine,
Sinks beaten by his chastisement below.
In the pale East the day peeps up its eye,
Changing from black to pallid blue the sky.
With Bernard and the War Witch there abide
Silence, and space, and breathless solitude.
Steadfastly she looks him in the face,
With eyes that swell at every word she speaks,
Till, like subduing suns, they glare the sky.

There are prime reasons why you must not yet

Cease to become my Bernard in the flesh.
Don't call your high vocation one of pain;
Though strife may come, grief shall not always reign.
There's something left for you to understand,
There's comfort for you on the lower land,
Where great events are waiting to unfold
Results whose magnitude remains untold.
Though some great wars that are to finish up
    The wreck of nations,
Must be fought while you are running over
    Mortal probations;
Yet shall you not be loser in the frays,
    Nor left repining;
The changing scenes that grow out of the days
    By war's refining,
Shall gladden all the future of the earth,
And hail the changed expediency of arms;
For better times shall find a happy birth,
And settled peace replace all past alarms;
No more shall kings plot battles, sense shall come
From the remainder, when the ciphering's done.

END OF CANTO II.

1

CANTO III.

"Lo! where the Giant on the mountain stands,
His blood-red tresses deep'ning in the sun,
With death-shot glowing in his fiery hands,
And eye that scorcheth all it glares upon;
Restless it rolls, now fix'd, and now anon
Flashing afar,—and at his iron feet
Destruction cowers to mark what deeds are done;
For on this morn three potent nations meet,
To shed before his shrine the blood he deems most sweet."
Byron.

BERNARD was safely landed upon the Spanish coast, a soldier, ready to do a soldier's work. England was out of sight, and scenes and friends familiar were now sensibly departed. The word " Forward " soon caused every soldier's joint to bend to its fate, while the band in front, always jovial, opened to the thrilling strains of "March to the Battle-field." Bernard found that he had to perform a very long and trying march indeed, which occupied many days, without remission. He was, however, at length actually engaged with the enemy; and, for the first time in his life, saw hundreds of his fellow-creatures laid prostrate by the hurled messengers of death; and learnt, from real experience, the ultimate duties of a soldier.

> Life is fancy's curse;
>   Death is fancy's slumber;
> Peace is fancy's nurse;
>   And battle fancy's thunder.

> But pain's sharp fancy gallops and stamps,
> And plays a thousand vinegar pranks
> About the brow, the lip, and the eye,
> And paints a ghost when it's going to die.

> What a frightful thing that fancy is,
>   When it's going to fancy no more!
> I'd almost never have fancied at all,
> Since a corpse I must come to after all.
> The beginning is great, but the end is small
>   Of that life whose sure death we deplore.

After passing through many severe conflicts and vicissitudes of the Peninsular war, it fell to Bernard's lot to be numbered with the veterans who were already attacking, for the last time, the hitherto impenetrable fortress of Badajos. " I shall not fall," he exclaimed, in a moment of excited rapture; " I shall not fall; she will be there, and England shall triumph."

To live and conquer enemies, is to live; all other life is death. Does any one imagine that soldiers have no feeling? Sensation glows with every trigger pulled; and every sword raised high makes counter-motions in as many hearts. Who feels the victory so much as those who earn it—who rush on bayonet-tops, climb frightful counterscarps, and in the torrent of every invented missile hurled, move on to gain or die?

Another day's march is over, and the fifth day of April, 1812, is passing into the oblivion of time used up. Bernard, with his regiment, has joined the investing army, under Wellington, which has just counted its nineteenth day of hard work upon that frowning fortress. There are its battlements, bastions, and embrasures, all visible under the light of the moon, while the quiet night, brooding its mantle over the surrounding scenery, brings a last living repose to fated thousands.

Now soldiers take rest for a few short hours;
   Sit down at your ease on the ground.
These moments enjoy that silence devours—
   To-morrow they will not be found!

The morrow came; it had an appalling birth, but the War Witch held in her hand the fate of its uproar. Invisibly she stood between the living and the dying, sheltering her love. At her nod a thousand balls took no effect, and at her desire they slaughtered.

The day advanced—the battle increased—cannon on
cannon blazed, and fury flowed in blood! Earth
drank the reeking moisture, while England, with her
curbless will, accosted pride's ambition, and on a
tyrant's throat held firm her angered arm!

Clamour and pain are struggling high,
Ten thousand noises rend the sky!
Soldiers, dashing to and fro,
Scarcely know which way to go.
Veiled in smoke the fortress throws
Showers of metal on its foes;
And tugs, and roars, and snorts, and moans,
From all its battle-planted stones,
And British flesh defies!

Fight on, ye French, give fire and cheer;
    These sons of home will yield.
They'll never stand when they come near
    The walls of your strong shield.

Work death so fast, that when they see
    Their gasping comrades low,
They'll hold a trembling truce to thee
    To let them safely go.

And should they dare to venture on
    Those frightful bulwarks high;
Then you can match them hand to hand,
    And merrily hail the sky.

Terrible to look at, mournful to tell,
Was that destructive siege ! On either side
Heroes were dying fast, whose latest words
No mortal ear could listen to ! Vengeance
Displaced humanity, and the din roar
Of passion liberated, reigned supreme !
The sides of the Leviathan gave way—
A breach yawned in the adamantine heights ;
And where the British iron entered first
Went British feet and British hearts alive !
But death dashed down that venturous "hope forlorn !"
And every tongue that cheered in that first batch
Left other tongues to tell their services.
Did this slight twitching of his ruffled mane
Dismay the " Lion," who was growing warm ;
Whose eyes were now wide open on his foe,
Measuring his work, and looking for a leap ?
Behold his final spring—his earnestness !
Full roused, he rushes to that venturous crush
He hates to take, but when he takes—O heavens !
The world can scarcely stand it !

Across their dying comrades down, they cheered,
And fell to die. Still gorged the tempting breach—
Still life o'er death climbed fast. The ladders went—
The scaling ladders dashed up hard against
The walls that rained forth hail-stones that fetched
    blood !

This was the hour that tried the sterling worth
Of each belligerent—the strain for victory!
The blood-streams on the battlements are seen,
As smoke drifts past the scarlet-sweating pile.
The ladders back are hurled by hands expiring;
Up again they go, contested sorely,
For those who raise them are prepared to die,
But will not die one breath before they must.
Their noble hearts have put their valour forth,
And now no earthly enemy can shake
Their dreadful resolution!

Lo! from a sulphureous cloud emerged,
Stands Bernard on the gory parapet!
His ladder fell not, yet no other man
Went safe the distance through.   Alone he stands—
Hat lost, sword raised, eyes turned to heaven up.
'Twas but a moment's look, and what he said
Was said to heaven; earth could not hear the words.

At this juncture the fate of the day turned in
favour of British arms.   A panic had seized the
French, and many guns of the enemy were suddenly
deserted.   These were taken possession of by the
invaders, and vigorously turned upon the vanquished,
enabling a strong body of our soldiers to gain the
fortress, and follow up the attack into the very core
of the citadel.   And then the work of hand-to-hand
displayed its sad severity.

Gorgeous scenes of blood profuse !
All sprinkled here, and spilt
By passion under guidance !
'Tis something here to live,
But little here to die !
Who fights and lives with limbs and eyes unsmashed,
Is favoured, and becomes
A walking spectacle of luck.
Who dies, might still worse fate have met,
In cold and lingering life,
And spectre-clad disease.

In battle, man discovers what he is ;
Dormant thoughts and feelings that had slept
Unroused since ever he disparted from
His mother's womb, awake.
Life, at every throb of his excited pulse,
Twinkles its whole ;
And all its keen intensity revolves
Ten thousand times before his burning eyes.
Early forgotten sins turn over
The leaves of their black registry.
Then, O then, how much he'd give
For but five minutes of repentance !
Affections rise, and coil their innate stings
Around his quick bewilderment,
Swell largely through his beating heart,
And make it ache beneath the cannon's roar
To native tenderness.

Yes, all these feelings do indeed possess
    The managed man of war;
And while he hacks the joints and marrow
    Of the foe,
And stabs and cuts the furious brows
Of stern and hardy enemies,
And walks upon the throats and straining eye-balls
    Of the groaning slain,
He thinks and feels like this—like this earns victory!

What screams are those that mingle with the night,
Whose dreary shades have now begun to lower;
    While guns quite mute lay sterwn
    With all the wreck they made?
    What are those new-born woes
    That try the soul of God?
    That make this day expire
    In groans, instead of praise?
    What are those hideous yells that shake
    The unaffected firmament,
    And cry to heaven in vain?

All ye whose true hearts feel, whose pure eyes read,
Whose minds despise immoral chastisements,
Unpublish all the doings of that night—
That hellish night of scarlet ire on earth!
For God's non-interference, to Himself
Let that great God account, whose ways are not
As our ways, and whose thoughts are very deep.

The wreck of man is ended with the day,
And now the wreck of woman is begun !
That blood which in heroic unity
Swelled forth to gain the stubborn citadel,
Is not allowed to cool, but left at large,
To be subdued on virtuous sacrifices !

Tell it no more !
Sinful stars twinkle no more !
Presumptuous moon, smile thou no more on me,
That knows this story to be true.
Spiritless sun, cover thyself with shame,
Or through a mantle shine, of that red blood,
Whose flow thou wouldst not stop !
Return thy reelings, callous earth,
Undo thy orbit, and retreat
With nature all reversing back again ;
Recall the time, and undo these aspersions
That besmear thy thousand beauties with disgust.
Then to me thou mayest justly
Shine and twinkle, smile, and gaily go
Through thy accuseless changes ;
And I will daily praise, and love,
Adore, and worship thee.

Bernard fought out the day unscathed, and at its
conclusion felt a new existence. After a battle, who
can tell, but those who have been there, how warriors
feel ? When all that was hazarded has passed through

E

the ordeal of the fiercest opposition, life seems re-made
—the world re-created.

Oh ! spare our lives, protect our honour !
And all our valuables—our money,
Houses, jewels—everything else shall be yours.
We will provide you every comfort here,
Of rest, refreshment, every joy we hold
Within our conquered dwellings we'll bestow,
And with our hands attend you thankfully—
Breathe blessings on yourselves and your relations,
If you but spare our virtue ; oh but spare
That which the world could never more repair !
Soldiers of England, let not your brave hearts
Be callous to the prayers of those who pray ;
The feeble ask your mercy, for your will
Is all the law that's left us under heaven.
Seize not these sacrifices, but proclaim
For us protection in this hour of pain.

Comrades and soldiers, what ! are there then
        none,
None to be found amongst our cloth, willing
To forego these temptations, and convey
Unsullied glory back to England's shores,
That in the British crown the blazing name
Of Badajos may shine a diadem ?
Or shall we prove our hasty selves to be
Much greater foes to these inhabitants

Than those who made their bondage limited;
And drive redeemless, through all future years,
The curse of our licentiousness?
Oh! in the name of all our Christian homes,
And all our quiet families at rest,
Where no intruder dare molest their peace,
Who now would check us if they knew our thoughts,
And chide us down to mercy with their tears,
If here they stood,—if here their voice could come!
Yield, yield, and gain a double victory!
But more, my comrades, more—much more than this;
Have you forgotten that the bravest hearts
Contain the largest honour, and should not
Require to be wrought upon by such stuff
As sermons, sighs, and sympathetic fears?
Where there's lack of honour, the glory won
Sounds like a bell that's cracked, and every time
The beastly thing is rung it pains the ear.

Revolting as the rapacity was, it is some consola-
tion to know that a few gallant heroes were found
worthy of their name, who, in the passions' tempest
of that distressing night, shielded helpless families,
and from imploring females kept off the hands of the
destroyer. Bernard Alvers joined one of these mag-
nanimous bands, and under a feeling of conscious
rectitude, prompted by well-taught moral obligations,
he passed that night in thankfulness to his Maker for
having preserved him for such inestimable services.
Don La Blass was once the wealthy possessor of the

mansion which Bernard, conjointly with several others, undertook to defend; and which charge, to the redeeming honour of the British army be it told, they did not violate. Don La Blass had fallen in defending his country. His estates, which were extensive, were now held in possession by three surviving daughters, their mother having died shortly after she received the news of her husband's death. One of these young ladies in particular, in her cries for mercy to the infuriated soldiers, excited unbounded compassion in the breast of Bernard. Her wild looks and earnest supplications, united with such superior gracefulness of person, and uttered with such dignified and persuasive language, took fast hold of Bernard's heart. He felt that it would be not only a duty, but a happiness to him, to die in her defence; and this, to her great joy, he told her he would do. Eleven others along with Bernard determined on guarding the house until the plunder should cease, and on these terms they were soon made the happiest guests in the world, and served with the choicest repast the mansion could afford. It was mutually arranged that six at a time of the twelve soldiers should take rest while the other six watched. They were all necessarily much fatigued, and drew lots to decide their turns. Thus passed the first night with Bernard Alvers in the conquered fortress of Badajos. Bernard, always fortunate, was one of the six who won the first sleep; and such a sumptuous bed as he found prepared for him he had not for a long time set eyes upon or ventured into.

It was a night—a woeful night, in which
The vilest vengeance dealt remorselessly
The wilful doom of death! With her legions
The War Witch hovered o'er the citadel,
And souls departing to eternal fates
She there disposed of variously.
Around the mansion of La Blass she threw
Her guardian eyes; she never left him once.
Waking or sleeping, all his passing hours
She got between; and as he slumbered there
She beckoned to his spirit through his clay.
The soul of the warrior then arose!
He knew the voice, he sees her once again;
She takes his hand, they mount the sulphury air,
Where, black with war's declining smoke, and rent
With screams, and shouts, and dying pains,
They view the hell below!

WAR WITCH.

Bernard, I have only the shadow of your spirit
here, whose essence still mingles with a corruptible
body. I must not therefore make impressions to
disqualify that union, which has not yet arrived at
the time or circumstance to become separated. But
I will dwell upon a few facts to teach you something
of man, and a little about gods. Do not be surprised
if my account of human actions should be at variance
with ordinary opinions. I regard no dogmatic cus-

toms, and deal with all things as they are. Knowing everything intuitively, gods require no learning, and our knowledge is as penetrative as our power is potent. Look below us, and see what severe affliction aches beneath the unbound devil, man. In all the species of animal life extant upon your bountiful and picturesque world, saw you ever such mad debauchery attempted ?

BERNARD.

Never! nor did my carnal dreams in their lewdest liberty ever portray such baseness. I shudder, not only at these red-hot rioters, but also at myself, because I also am human. Within my own veins there must dwell the latent rage that this scene illustrates! Would that I could run the purple gore all off, and refill the channels with some milder, purer liquid, changing my capability of such contingent danger to a virtuous and moral consummation.

WAR WITCH.

Yes, your nature embraces the violative mischief, but in suppressible proportion. Qualities of mind you have that keep this demon down. These were your birth-gift; I saw them shared to you, and ever with my constant blessing have I nourished them.

BERNARD.

Then I am surprisingly favoured ; made man, and saved from his extreme delinquencies. This explains to me something of what I have frequently felt; which is, a conscious relation to a presence not emanating from man, yet emanating from or contained in all other natural things. For, ever with the soaring changeful clouds, the setting sun's rejoicements, the mountain stream's clear melodies, my soul mingled attachment. These always seemed to requite my affection. With everything but man I always enjoyed sweet fellowship. He only, in the mighty theatre of things outspread, appeared to be the stranger! When the songsters of the woods poured forth unnumbered welcomes to my wandering footsteps, when the stars of evening twinkled me "good night," or when the moon danced to my eyes in her true and liberal smiles, he only spoke in anger, he only seemed to envy me that joy which heaven and nature never did refuse.

WAR WITCH.

That, in man, which seemed to envy you the pleasure of your own inoffensive existence, is now, through its perversion, driving him into the doomed chambers of Badajos, and urging him on to the destruction of others' peace, others' lives, and others' virtue. It is that sensitive but inordinate propensity in him called selfishness!—that mighty passion of his nature which the world cannot satisfy—the universe cannot surfeit! The viciousness of selfishness is its sin; that sin, however, is very early developed, and through life its banefulness grows with its exercise. And should an awful hour ever come, as it now has, to unchain the fetters of

restricting law, and let the tiger loose, he springs
to rapine, dives into guideless plunder, and re-
exhibits the savage he was tamed from.

BERNARD.

I must admit that selfishness appears to be the
incentive to the evil now going on; but surely something nobler than that vile thirst headed the torrent
of the late battle? What! has this fortress been
conquered without a sense of national or personal
honour; and has man no dignified or loyal motives?

WAR WITCH.

Man, undoubtedly, does possess motives of the
highest order and praiseworthiness; but in what
manner, I shall presently explain. First I must tell
you that all his motives to action, whether those
actions be moral or immoral, honourable or disrepu-
table, spring from selfishness. A man may appear
to forego a pecuniary temptation for the sake of his
honour, but it must be remembered that his sense of
honour in such a case is more acute than his love of
gold. He yields to the stronger impulse, the operation of which is the result of his constitution or
education. He may perform large acts of charity,
but for what? To gain a name? Such is frequently
the case; but I will deal more liberally with him
now, and assume that he yields only to the dictates
of pure benevolent feelings; and gives, unseen by
the world, a good proportion of his wealth to the
afflicted and indigent. Private fervent prayers, along

with this world's goods, may also be offered up, and all done with disinterested Christian love, from the single principle of selfishness. Man is his own sweet idol, and his own soul is his god, under every denomination of thought and action—yesterday, to-day, and for ever!

BERNARD.

Where then do you place virtue? Is there no such thing? no difference of quality between actions? Are they only the accidental results of individual peculiarities? Are all as blameless as they are commendable, and is there no absolute distinction between evil and good?

WAR WITCH.

It is hard to make man admit the naked truth, or believe the nature of his own heart. The very property I have explained operates against it; and he keeps his adorable slave, Pride, to whip the truth away. It is a busy slave, that Pride: the impudent and inseparable correlative of his dangerous aspirations. Actions have a wide distinction, though they are all based in the natures which it has pleased the Almighty to call into existence. Their direct manifestations result either from passions or motives. Passions and motives, which keep in operation the whole of the animal creation, are both continually dispensing good and evil. Motives to action may be said to belong more exclusively to man; passions, more generally, to the brutes. Good and moral motives modify and subdue the evils that the passions prompt, which ruling power brutes do not possess. But vicious motives, if not kept in restraint by external law, inflame the passions, make man a human devil, and urge him to commit deeds beyond the power or desire of instinctive brutes. Look, Bernard, beneath us, and own the truth of my assertion.

BERNARD.

Happy is he whose motives aspire to fame, and not to infamy!

WAR WITCH.

You perceive then why brutes are incapable of fermenting such a turmoil of riot, sin, and shame as this in Badajos; which makes all heaven ache to breathe upon it?

BERNARD.

Yes, and I perceive him there, the early made lord of the creation, sunk far beneath his servants—the cattle that feed upon the mountains. May I inquire if the greater or lesser portion of the human family are infected with these commandless desires? Because if the majority are so, we must rank our race below the brutes. If the majority are of the better motive class, then, and then only, can we rank ourselves above those animals; for, to strike a comparative value for our species, we must determine the average of its qualities.

WAR WITCH.

Right you are—pushing the subject in the proper direction, and soon we shall discover as much as it will be useful for you to know, and solve the unwelcome problem of man's selfishness. The fact of man possessing mind, raises him at once very high above the brutes; for he is thereby endowed with a dilution of that true spirit possessed in perfection by the gods. Man is a combination of deity and flesh. Mind, when first installed in human organism, produced a new phenomenon; and matter, with this mysterious force, went almost frantic. It was a modern species tied to heaven and earth, and destined to display, in the school of experience, its hitherto untested qualities. Up to the period that we now converse, each flying day has pushed it in advance ; progressively it moves, both individually and in the mass, enjoying selfishness.

BERNARD.

Does man really possess within him anything akin to the perfection of Deity ? This admission raises him wonderfully in my estimation, and inclines me almost to consider it a virtue to be selfish; since, to serve and worship ourselves, we must necessarily worship something of our Maker.

WAR WITCH.

Another step into truth—another link of evidence produced. Oh there are truths and wonders in your constitution, which, if I were suddenly to unfold to you, your soul would burst its little bounds, and drive your flesh to atoms! But such amazements are reserved, to be disclosed gradually to probationary mortals, the work of many generations yet to come.

BERNARD.

If man is so gifted, with a quality so perfect, how is it that his selfishness is so obviously misdirected?

WAR WITCH.

Though in its primitive and abstract state one quality he holds is infallible, in its human combination it is not so, but is thereby reduced to a comparatively passive condition, and subject to the influence of circumstances. A field is herein open for the permissive speculations of all the minor deities, whose incessant employment is to control the great human family. Opposed to our benevolent struggles for man's welfare, are not only the wild propensities of his own passions, but also the vigilant assailments of crafty, fallen spirits, who strive to emulate us in the traffic of souls. For wise purposes man is born into the world subject to these two conflicting powers, by which he is tried and proved.

BERNARD.

Under all these influences, whatever course he chooses to pursue, is he invariably contributing to one paramount craving—selfishness?

WAR WITCH.

Yes, his devotion to self either saves or damns him. If he adheres to an evil course, his spirit, when it leaves his body, becomes a fallen one. If, on the other hand, he adopts an upright and religious life, faithful to the end, the same shall be saved. You hold many diverse opinions on earth about fallen spirits and angels. Some of the best of men have held very false notions; but, the tenaciously adhering, for want of more perfect disclosures, to what they conscientiously believed, was in them a virtue, and not a fault. Harmless errors are less objectionable than pernicious ones, and far less objectionable than pernicious practices; and almost any doctrine that tends to curb sordid indulgences, to establish social and family affections, to forgive injuries, and promote peace, is a blessing to mankind, though it be mingled with error. If the mind of a man grows vitiated, he delights to satisfy his lust; in doing which, he pleases himself, and thereby worships the devil. If the mind of a man becomes purified from evil, and by exercising the more noble sense and sentiments of moral rectitude he finds the greatest pleasure, he frames his conduct accordingly, and thereby pleases himself, and worships God.

BERNARD.

But might he not worship God from a disinterested motive, or rather from a sense of religious duty, more than from a selfish desire? And is he not capable of enjoying some forbidden pleasures? And does he

not shun them, not because they are distasteful, but
from the fear of incurring the penalty of the indulgence ?

WAR WITCH.

Man worships God from a sense of duty, so far
only as that sense agrees with his own desires, and
consequently not from disinterested motives. Self is
at the bottom of the act. He is also capable of
enjoying many forbidden pleasures, and shuns them
only because his mind is more keen to the conse-
quences of the participation, than it is to the transi-
tory enjoyment they afford. He calculates, and finds
that the final loss would be to him greater than the
present gain, and gives to self the benefit. All love
in heaven and on earth is also kindled and sustained
by such tendencies. Does it lower me anything in
your estimation to tell you that it is to please myself
I love you? God is worshipped by this single principle
in his sinless and holy heaven, and He himself established the motive in order that He might be sought
after with the purest sincerity. What is love of
country but selfishness? Every man thinks his own
land better than his neighbour's, and such a feeling
can never wholly forsake him. No bribery, no compact, could make him fight for others with that
native courage with which he fights for his own. No
earthly value could estrange the honest heart from
the soil upon which it first began to beat, or
nationalise to foreign thrall its free and independent
birth. What is it that has civilised the nations but
selfishness? Your own country's refinements, its

wealth, its independence, and its power, are all the offsprings of innate selfishness. Selfishness civilises, monopolises, and misanthropises. Selfishness toils in its longings till it vanquishes its own existence. Inordinate and insatiable, it flings its very breath as fuel to its own passion, and dies greedy of the last spark that proclaims its annihilation!

BERNARD.

May I ask what are the future prospects of the world in regard of war? What the ultimate conduct of man with man's affairs? Will ever there reign upon the earth universal and abiding peace?

WAR WITCH.

If you wish to understand the true principles of national and legislative establishments, and require a standard by which to calculate on probable and popular changes, you possess it in yourself. The lesson is simple, but nevertheless important. The mass mingles together the same interests and effects as those that influence a single individual, being homogeneous. Understand therefore yourself, and you may then fairly judge of all. If you find it difficult to understand and judge correctly of the world's great movements, infer that it is also difficult to understand and to know yourself. Watch and think, and when you do so, remember that thousands do the same to no advantage. There is a periodicity in every thing, feeling, and event, common to all existences. There's not a breath escapes the lips of

man but is so governed; there's not a pulse obeys
the laws of circulation, but publishes the fact; and
every feeling of the mind contains the immutable
attribute, which, ere man was made, existed in the
unavoidableness of his advent and his destiny, whose
selfishness now works through its evil periods into
the tedious but sure perfection of his fate.   But,
Bernard, you cannot know one millionth part of all
the changes and returns of organised development;
nor will it be necessary for you or me to wait to see
the end.   A generation, yea, the lifetime of a world,
but just fills up some gap that yawns between!

My mission on this time-refining world shall close
when you are ready for my final vow.   Then other
prompters from above, and other actors down below,
shall carry on the forging of the chain which time
links on to lives and history.

> To heaven's fair hills I steal,
>   Away, away;
> Where no dull minutes feel
>   A dying day.

> Love waits on you below,
>   Awake, awake;
> I've settled matters so,
>   Therefore partake.

Shall I tell what it was that awoke him from slumber?
A kiss on his lips and a stroke on his brow.
" Kind soldier, brave soldier, you have slept through
    the number
Of hours allotted for reposing in now."

It was Julia La Blass that stood by his bed-side,
And she declared him her bodily saviour;
For it was he that had saved her from shame's ruth-
    less tide,
So she worshipped his noble behaviour.

And she prayed for his sake and her own whilst he
    slept,
And she moistened with weeping his pillow;
And she secretly there made a vow, which she kept,
To depart with her love o'er the billow.

JULIA.

Oh! ye immortal powers, whose secret will
Unfolds itself in Time's abrupt events,
Is this the crisis of my mortal life—
The pinnacle on which my lot must turn—
The port in which my bark, tossed by foul winds,
Is destined to lie still? Then, welcome, fate!
The difference might have been more shameful!
Unclose those very heavy lids of thine,
Important stranger, that from thine own
Expressive lips I may at once receive

F

Welcome or woe.   Oh! blessed night for me,
If in his soul there lives what on his face
Is to my eyes revealed.   Impatient heart,
Hold your longing; soon he must arise ;—
To wake him up would be to rob myself,
For he must leave this chamber, and another
Take his place.   With him I'll stay or go—
With him, and only him, through all this night
I'll battle through the dangers of the siege.
This is no time for custom ; the doomed world
Is poising on its last momentous die ;
These rushing moments now may purchase years,
Ill-gotten wealth, or quick eternity !
Heaven and hell are going very cheap ;
What matters then one woman !

> Discretion, this is love—leave me.
> I'm engaged for self and fate ;
> And every morrow of my life
> Hangs on my present state.

BERNARD (*awaking*).

Good heavens! where am I ?—I thought I was a
fighting soldier, and desperately fighting at the siege
of Badajos; but .I have been so much under the
influence of dreams that I find it very difficult sometimes to discern whether I am really asleep or awake.
—This must be still a dream !

JULIA.

Soldier of England, have you forgotten, in your short but necessary sleep, how and why you became thus situated?

BERNARD.

Fair lady, I did forget, but I am now awake to sense. War's rare fortune smiles upon me again in this most precious circumstance. Did I earn the glory I am crowned with in the battle-field?

JULIA.

If you feel it glory to be here, you did achieve it by your conduct in the battle.

BERNARD.

Incomparable woman! you have been sleeping, like myself, with the gods; and your angelic eyes dart rapture into mine, throwing off their heavenly influence.

JULIA.

May they continue in such employment
For ever, if 'for ever' lives in love;
And what can claim eternity but love?—
Which keeps its life up with its consciousness—
Never at rest, but swelling in progression?
If God, who is all love, grows in His joy,
When will he burst this happy universe?

BERNARD.

Not before the secret of my soul
Bursts to the sweet oppressiveness you fling
Around me in devouring language.
Oh! on the evening's gentlest languishing,
On summer's sultry sighs, or˙o'er the hills,
Stealing in mellow sounds music's soft notes,
There never came such heart-researching tones,
To court my now emancipated ears.
This world's perfection fails before their strength,
Which, rushing upward from this sphere of dust,
Soar on to heaven, to find a counterpart.

JULIA.

Your words have supercharmed all mine, unhinged
Their little strength, dispersed their vapoury sounds;
And, like the warmer sun upon the dew,
Absorbed their cold and fleeting frailty.

BERNARD.

Fair speaker, you have garlanded my eyes
With insecure refulgence; to their view
A graspless diadem you have held up,
That, not for me, in distance magnifies.
Yet so vivid are its cheating charms,
That fancy fain would try and snatch at it;
But wretched reason weeps to feel the lie,
And, chastening, stamps down fancy's vanity.

JULIA.

Oh, no ! If these poor eyes of mine to yours
Good service make ; if on thine ear this voice—
This weak and worthless voice—breaks pleasingly ;
If these prompt hands can find acceptance too ;
And if this trembling heart, that I am scarcely
Mistress of, which aches in joy beneath
Thy searching gaze, can only meet in thine
A kindred glow ; accept their mutual offerings,
Which now to thee I freely make complete,
With all their worldly goods entitled to.

BERNARD.

Pray think again before you thus conclude.
Would you accept a soldier rude, like me,
To be your heart's companion all through life ?
Me, so humbly reared, and so untaught
In all the favoured privileges
And customs of advanced society ?
An alien to politeness, speech, and rank,
To which estate, more favoured, you are native ?

JULIA.

These are not faults, and if indeed they were,
Love draws a veil of full perfection there.
Were all the learning of encumbered lore
Infused through thee, it could not in my eyes
Increase their love of yours. What's rank to me ?
Or rhetoric's rules ? or grave philosophy ?

When all my veins are smarting and inflamed—
Bursting with hot impatience to receive
One word of hope, one sentence of despair !
In my distressed, in my devoted sight,
The riches of this world are poverty—
The veriest trash that ever tried to please.
Oh ! such vague objections constitute
A secret dread of something unexpressed.
Lurks there a foe between my heart and thine ?
Am I too late to win for life's content
The gem that toils my soul with dazzling ?
Such wretched bliss I never underwent,
Such shocks of love, such tempest-thoughts as these !

BERNARD.

Raise up again those sudden downcast eyes,
Give me once more that latest look you threw,
Which in my heart sunk deep—is sinking still.
No more despair ; I will be what you ask.
Unknown, unloved I am by womankind,
Save that maternal love which binds through life
A mother to her son.   She claims me still,
But only to increase her happiness
And yours, by blessing us together,
As we thus in mutual concert vow.
But let me warn you that my trade is war,
That nothing finds adversity so fast ;
Its triumphs and rewards resemble much
The sunny days of winter—short and few.

The scheme is of necessity made up,
And Death pays many a man his wages.

JULIA.

Then you shall be his creditor for life.
Leave your account with me, and I'll tell Death
You fought for love, and have been paid;
And fought enough to warrant settlement;
But as He could not liquidate your claim,
Julia La Blass pays up the full amount.
Thus victory ends your hardships in the field;
Harsh war has climaxed into perfect love;
And through a dark and dreadful journey we
Are landed in a perfect paradise.

She kept her vow; she claimed him for herself,
Unconscious of the War Witch, who knew all;
But whose engagement was not to prevent
The full enjoyment on the earth below
Of all that man is made for in his day.
The War Witch was the chooser of this bride—
A perfect bride for her predestined love.
For in the future largeness of estate,
Where all is nothing but excessive soul,
The recollection of completed peace
In all the flesh required, makes satisfied
The spirit that has passed the narrow gates
Of small mortality, where, fully served,

Wants that repast no more, and only longs
For all the unexpired newness that comes,
To still come on to eyes unturned,—to sense,
All pacified behind, but not before ;
Where every throw is fresher than the last,
That, lovely, swells upon the joyous surge
That bathes the spirit with eternity.

Bernard Alvers became the happy spouse of Julia
La Blass, who accompanied him to his native village,
where they both spent the remainder of their days ;
and Julia, equally happy, found all her highest hopes
realised by being united to the only man she ever
loved, or ever desired to love, fulfilling to Bernard,
for his own sake, the promise of the War Witch
when she said to him—

" I will send you pleasures many,
Of all earth's sons the most of any."

END OF CANTO III.

CANTO IV.

"He gave his honours to the world again,
His blessed part to Heaven, and slept in peace."
Shakespeare.

'TWAS at the hour when day begins to dream,
And feathered songsters, through the pleasant
    groves,
Sing to his rest the swelling sun;
When o'er the earth appearances and tones,
In mellowed beauty, sanctify the season;
When rivulets softly break their bubbles,
Echoing on the evening's stillness,
And the mountain-goat's faint bleat is heard
Across the empty valley as it dims;
The quiet hour when labour languishes,
And man, upon the night's chill breeze,
Sighs off the day's fatigue.   Thus was it then;—
The nearest tide to Bernard's village did
Begin to turn its flood, and the full moon
With meek but brilliant face, began to pry

Round all the corners of the wheeling world,
Which had become so tranquil, so composed,
That heaven reclined its blissful spirit down,
And rested on the scenery.

At that calm epoch was there still alive,
Though in subdued obedience to some power,
The principle of rage ?   Was passion then
Delivered up from all terrestrial things—
The flesh of man—the tempest of the air—
And threatenings of the dread volcano's throat ?
Was all at rest to be disturbed no more ?
Was earth a speechless monument—a tomb
Of beauty covering its own dead strife ?

Ah no ! no, no,
Things were not so ;
And cannot—shall not
Ever be so ;
For the world was made
To roll and change,
And all that exists
Requires a change—
Demands a change ;
And there's no good life
Without a change—
No pleasure, no contentment.

The eyes without moving
　　Could never feel joy;
The blood without moving
　　Would soon become dry;
And the sky without changing
Would set us all raging,
　　And longing to die.

The night and the day,
　　The heat and the cold,
The mournful, the gay,
　　The pious, the bold,—
Are changes that keep us alive,
Conditions in which we all thrive,
　　Beneath a ficklesome sky.

Hark! a solemn sound—a note of sadness
Breaks on the stillness of this dying day!
Night's calm anticipation is disturbed;
Fate knocks at slumber-closing lids, and cries
" Awake! to celebrate a spirit's destiny."

This sound is Bernard's village knell,
That never spoke before to tell
　　Of such a soul departed!
The consternation is the woe
That dear relations feel below,
When Death strikes down his heavy blow,
　　And makes them broken-hearted.

And more than this; not earth alone
Is stirred at what Death now has done
    To rob the English nation ;
But Heaven, with all its deathless train,
The flying soul to entertain,
    Is making preparation.

And while the knell sends through the air
    Its voice of solemn woe ;
While o'er his yet warm corpse bends she,
Fond Julia, drowned in agony,
Whose eyes scarce through the flood can see
    What she can scarce forego ;

While neighbours round the village weep,
In anguish that has driven sleep
    From every streaming eye ;
While for their father's sake they press,
In grief's mistakeless earnestness,
    His numerous family ;

While aged eyes and young ones smart
    Together in one wail,
And mix the woe they cannot part,
Searching and sinking through each heart ;
    Deep sounds fly through the gale !

Again, deep sounds fly through the gale !
    The weather broods a storm !

The scared inhabitants turn pale,
And suffer an alarm.

The threatening sky
Is raging high,
With noises and commotion ;
The moon turns dim,
The stars go in,
Lightning flashes,
Thunder crashes,
And storm afflicts the ocean !

" Just dead on earth,"
A voice cries from above ;
" Receiving birth
In heaven for endless love."

" Come forth, come forth," it cries aloud,
" Come from your earthly tomb and shroud,
To endless freedom rise ;
I've waited long, must have you now,
To satisfy my early vow ;
To me this night brings joy !
Bequeathed to me by Heaven's will,
I'll comfort and defend you still,
Throughout eternity."

Thus spoke the War Witch, as she came
Downwards with a glittering train,

Shining through the night;
All the village gazers trembled
At this host of souls assembled,
As they viewed the sight.

She duly reached the earth he had to leave,
Just as his spirit o'er the cooling clay
Lingered to say farewell.   Nothing it now knew,
Save its dropped conservatory, but life.
Eternity's commencement—the broad stage
A naked soul feels lost at suddenly,
And trembling waits for judgment to be passed.

The infernal regions at this juncture roared,
And dared once more to start its armies forth!
The mustering fiends began to look about
For one more chance to dash at victory!
But all the space between their condemned bounds,
And where he died, was strongly fortified
With tribes the fiends had been defeated by.
Thus disappointed, in their lake they laved,
Venting forth rage on hot upheaving flames.

And now, behold how brightly shines the bride,
That fresh from heaven comes laden with desire
To consummate a union, that must last
As long as stars shall stand within their place,
Or suns make worlds form orbits round their glare;
A union that no future law can break,

No life can limit, and no death can part;
A joining without fear, not of false hands,
Not of feigned lips and bright dissembling eyes,
That cloak the fearful secrets of the heart,
Of which base blood and flesh are capable.
For here the art deceptive cannot play;
Mud to mud is gone—no covering clogs
The pure transparent evidence of truth,
That soul to soul displays. Perfection beams
In contrast with the passages of sin.
Undying life contended through below.
The trials over, all that's free's redeemed; ·
And free as is all heaven, so free is he
Who enters clear of all imputive crimes.

The War Witch now arranges her gay throng
In bridal order, like a garland spread
Through the whole sky's concave circumference;
This arch triumphal inlaid with such lips,
And spangled with such eyes, exceeds in glow
All earthly trials at skill—in majesty
Inscribes the universe! From the centre
Of this superb display the War Witch turns
To greet her bridegroom on his bridal morn.
· Her face comes round so gently with a smile,
As if she felt her happiness begun;
His presence tells upon her, and her looks
Flash forth imperial greetings through his soul.
Spirit meets spirit—all sight, all feeling,

Whose bliss intensifies the concord scene,
Till Heaven rings out with blessings on this pair.

O ye nations, with all your languages,
How vainly you afford the smallest means
Of naming for a moment what they felt.
The angels, overwhelmed, wept out their share
Of sympathy in tears, which sparkling fell
Like dew-drops on the bridegroom and the bride;
Relieved from this first shock, they tune their harps,
And usher in the brilliant wedding feast.

"O Love, Love, may you live
For ever in our sight!
While space retires through distance free
Our thousand lyres we'll sound to thee,
In all their festive might."

To individual form she calls him forth,
Once more to view him perfect and entire.
Obedient to her power, he then throws out
His shape celestial; formed but not corrupt.
Leaning still on him she courts his gaze,
Blesses him, ejaculates, rejoices.

WAR WITCH.

Joy here is not assumed—no counterfeit
Can dazzle in such fraud; all here is real:

Real as the light the sun cannot refuse,
When no obstruction stands before his blaze ;.
Real as the Maker who designed what is,
Who never will pervert His will revealed.
As it was, so it is, and for ever
Shall continue and abide with us.
Come now with me, but first look where you leave,—
There goes your earth, away from you for ever;
From us it flies, and reeling as it roves,
Its continents and seas display themselves;
See how the ball diminishes in size,
And how the faithful moon, her daughter, keeps
Her proper distance everlastingly;
Who, although she reels more tardily, still
Keeps up the chase, and travels twice as much.

BERNARD.

Loved earth, farewell! for I have done with thee,
Thou glorious planet of my birth;
Scene of my fortunes and my victories—
Farewell for ever!

WAR WITCH.

Bernard, you have not yet seen heaven; be calm,
In matter's attraction we wander still.
Turn, turn your eyes—behold! they come, they come!
A rush of globes! Move, move, and let them pass.
Hear you the noise they make, as space they cleave?

G

There flies Mars, followed by the asteroids,
All moonless and unmarried; so also
Are Venus and Mercury, who closer twine
Around that scorching luminary's ribs
Who claims their endless loyalty.
Look out! here comes the monster Jupiter,
Decked with his four resplendent satellites;
Make way for him, for he is powerful,
And the most gigantic of them all!
Nearing us, see how he blocks up space,
Obscuring every other world.   He comes—
He goes—and leaves us room again.
Now Saturn shines, and bids us both good-morrow;
This is a fanciful creature.   Observe
How he winds around his vainful majesty
A double golden ring, not satisfied
With eight times one of moons.   Wait till he comes,
And then, upon his burnished edges, we
Will both together bravely trespass there,
And trample curiosity threadbare.
Here he is—step in.   'Tis earth, 'tis solid earth
Unmountained.

BERNARD.

Majestic, without mountains!
Vision, the soul's telegraph, sends a sense
That, without sight, no mind could comprehend.
O let us, in the newness of this world,
Rove round and round upon his endless plain;

Now we are here, let's peep between his rings,
Walk in his many moons' conflicting shades,
And then the parent globe admire, and see
How all the universe appears from here,
A point I never viewed it from before.
O why was matter formed so uniform?
Why not more, like this piece, diversified?—
This grand departure from the common shape,
Which, to the primitive great universe,
Holds forth an elegant new fashion.

WAR WITCH.

Bernard, you are only brinking wonder,
And when with me you stem the further tide
Of current power, and dive where depthless space
No tangent gives, but yields and yawns for ever;
Then you will confess that fancy has done,
In some hands, its duty marvellously!

So come with me,
And life shall be,
A journey free,
    And a roomy race;
Fields of pleasure,
There shall measure
Out their treasure
    Of indulgent grace.

G 2

Away we fly,
We're driving high
Beyond the sky,
    Where argument fails;
We're bounding free,
Through nebulæ,
Where comets flee
    With fiery tails.

BERNARD.

Oh, stop this rush! Is this heaven's wilderness?
These increasing shades make me a stranger.
Warm up the vacancy with something close;
I cannot bear the stretch my spirit fills.
Yielding away I feel so coldly spread
Through such a length, that all my power fails
To gather up again together, my own
Unmanageable distribution.

WAR WITCH.

'Tis so with immortality—fear not;
As birth in flesh brings pain to breathe at first,
So birth in heaven seems first oppressive bliss;
There is a first but not a last of this;
The final first of every change is come.

Out shines again that myriad host of song,
Whose sudden beams, uniting into one,
Strengthen the marriage transports just begun.

First their blaze, and then their harps, and then
Their shrill multipled voices rend the heavens,
Like three devouring elements at work,
That make the void seem solid with delight.

" Invoke our will, for heaven's wide,
   Untiring still we'll stem the tide
      That rolls along through vacancy.
   We know no check, no bounds, no stay ;
   No darkness, no concluding day ;
   And all that lies within our way
      Is pleasure and complacency."

WAR WITCH.

Speak not of bliss—Oh ! name it something else.
Strike not for us, thus charged with whelming love,
For we indeed are lavishly supplied.
Turn round, and heave your vocal affluence
Into confineless distance ; there speak out
In love's alarm.   Call all the distant gods
And goddesses, who in their common joys
Weary out long eternity.   Disturb
Their quiet undertakings ; rouse their clans ;
Enjoin them to come down, a little down,
To see my bliss, and throw in sympathy
With me, to make this pleasure bearable.
Call !   Strike !   Alarm the concave galleries !

Silence, that on its tip-toe breathlessness
Had been a listener, now panting broke,

And as the lightning dashes not in time,
But pops between its strides, so, madly forth
Flies the obedience of the choristers.

Behold—heaven moves! and in its getting up
Shakes its unseen remotenesses.
Advancing hosts in endless crowds respond,
Who, in their rich descent, each other greet,
Commingling salutations. On they come,
Like a bright ocean of celestial waves,
Whose every undulation is a tongue
That moves through all one pulse that feels the same.

WAR WITCH.

" Brethren of our great empire in the skies "
(She speaks beneath the listenment of God,
Who high above all other spendour shines),   .
" To whose innumerable marriages
I have often lent my aid, and worshipped
At your happy nuptial shrines, now has come
Your turn to render blessing for blessing,
And celebrate, through all this gaze of eyes,
My happy virgin death, whose victory
Is the life which that sweet death confers."

Pronounce to us your pleasure ;
    Our hearts and tongues all wait
To strike in concord measure,
    And loudly celebrate

This new event that crowns us,
This passion that surrounds us.

And onward its dilation
  We will stretch in music's voice,
And bless this consummation
  Of your contented choice.

And love alive shall onward strive,
  With life that knows no measure,
And through the sway of termless day
  Far revel in its pleasure.

Silence recurs! Attention strings all eyes,
Spotting the heavens with fire! The War Witch,
Upraising all her utmost majesty,
Looks up above her million guests, and thus
Invokes the high and merciful Supreme:

Unborn first cause, and unbegotten self—
Almighty living power—creation's God!
In whose researching universal sight
Heaven's purity is alone sustained,
And kept from running into sin, which stains
All matter's sinful forms,—vouchsafe to hear
The words of Thy dependent minister,
Who now would dare to thank Thee for
My high appointment and permitted joys.
Over my soul goes no delight, but makes

A stronger sense of gratitude to Thee.
From Thee the buddings of my life came forth;
Then back again to Thee, its source, let all
Its happiness return, to live enthroned
Where pleasures cannot die.

The Godhead spreads His glory over her,
Accepting her just offering, and the scene
Thus manifested throws into unity
Contributory blessings from the throng.
Then up the veil ascends—the only veil
That separates the brightest realms from these—
For her grand entrance to completed bliss.
This opening up is for the War Witch made,
And her affianced partner, now made one.
A voice descending, richer than the scene,
Invites her to come up and occupy,
With him she loves, her everlasting home.

Embracing Bernard now, the War Witch claims
His future freedom from all fears and pains.
Directs his gaze to higher bliss in store,
And bids him dwell on earthly thoughts no more;
But vanquish grief where only love reclines,
And let the world jog on with its designs.
Confirmed in smiles that angels make and give,
Enjoy with her this rich estate, and live;
Enjoy with her, who had to wait so long,
This home of safety, liberty, and song. —

It's all secure!—and He who cannot change,
Gives thee and her this paradise to range.

. BERNARD.

Is this the end of mortal man redeemed ?
Th' estate of Adam's progeny reclaimed,
Though nearly lost ?   Superb possession !
O ! heights and depths, that beat conception
Clean out of existence, knowledge is here
As nothing !   And far beyond the pale
Of intellectual strides my eyes swim on
In one unbroken gaze !   My earthly love,
Beneath Almighty will, is here suppressed.
War Witch, I cannot ever weep again !
I'm too incapable, too strong with joy,
Too overloaded with redemption's flavour,
Too full of peace, to shed another tear !

WAR WITCH.

We stand upon the threshold of the prize
That millions from the earth have passed into,
But never yet across this threshold went
One woe to taint the purity within.
Hark ! the strains begin !   Advance with speed !
Into these welcomes dive—these silver sounds
Absorb us loving to infinity !

ANGELS ABOVE.

These tearless fields of light,
For you are beaming bright—
Are glowing, beaming bright.
This endless stretch of day,
For you shall shine and stay—
For ever shine and stay.

Hail! Bernard Alvers, hail!
Where joy and peace prevail
In God's essential home.
Come in, come on, go through
The portion kept for you,
All round about His throne.

Within that ocean of the sanctified,
Where no stray sin can mingle with the tide,
Glide on the happy pair; pressing softly,
Brightly forward into deepening glory;
Heralded with shouts those regions love—
Those regions only hear. The end was come;
The perfect hope was closed that lived so long—
That never flagged. In him, in her, the faith
That first had birth, continued steadfast
Under all conflictions. Alike they loved,
Alike they trusted and believed; and now,
Alike, they both are blessed for evermore.

THE END.

Songs.

SONGS ON THE LATE WAR
WITH RUSSIA.

WE ARE NOT FREE.

WAKE! arm! arm! give up your ease;
　None but the brave are free;
Hear you the warning voice each breeze
　Conveys across the sea?
Armed hosts obey the tyrant's will,
　His wide dominions rise,
Their war-clang makes the mountains thrill,
　And tremble to the skies!
We are not free, cannot be free,
　While such a foe is strong.
He threatens all that liberty
　Which we have loved so long.

Up! up! advance! drive sleep away,
　From England's eyes alarmed.
Rest not in freedom's battle-day
　Till Russia's pride's disarmed.
Lo! now the greedy despot stands,
　Fiend monarch of the earth!
His zealots dare to drench their hands
　In blood of British worth!
We are not free, cannot be free,
　While such a foe is strong;
He threatens all that liberty
　Which we have loved so long.

Dream, dream no more ; wait not to think,
  For every moment's wing
Adds to the chain another link
  His bloodhounds round us fling ;
They stain the ground—the earth is pained
  Beneath their trampling din.
Our ranks are thinned, our homesteads drained,
  Life sickens at their sin.
We are not free, cannot be free,
  While such a foe is strong.
He threatens all that liberty
  Which we have loved so long.

Come forth ! leave home ! tell every friend,
  However dear he be,
That peace is rushing to an end—
  The future, slavery !
That on the heights our foe, inflamed
  With wrath's malignant ire,
Makes thousands to his evils trained,
  Pour down consuming fire !
We are not free, cannot be free,
  While such a foe is strong ;
Then forth ! and save that liberty
  Which we have loved so long.

ENGLAND, ROUSE!

HAT is life? Come, let us give it
  For the freedom of the free ;
Not one moment would I live it
  If the terms mean slavery!
Then, England, rouse! the hour is nigh
When every valiant son must die,
    Or be a serf!

Up! up! you cannot longer slumber,
  Danger hovers o'er your sleep ;
The Russians our brave troops outnumber,
  Who, at home the Russians keep.
Then, England, rouse! let every hand
Rise for the freedom of that land
    Which gave it birth.

Hark! the sounds from thousands dying,
  Of the bravest of the brave!
Hark! at home relations sighing
  For their distant gory grave!
Then, England, rouse! thy sons who lie
Cold covered in first victory,
    Demand your aid.

Example in ripe glory shames you,
  If you hesitate to come ;

No false thought is safe that blames you
   To complete the work begun.
At once disclaim a Briton's name,
If your blood shuns a warrior's fame
   Or fears to flow.

THE YOUNG SOLDIER'S FAREWELL.

'VE been your son, dear father,
   For nearly twenty years;
And I could die now rather
   Than see your face in tears.
Don't weep—I cannot bear it,
   Yet I must go away;
There's war, and I must share it,
   It comes in my young day.
Hark! hark! the danger's on us;
   Screams of the dying tell
That peace has parted from us;
   Dear father, fare thee well!

Try to forget, dear mother,
   That I was ever thine,
And let your love some other
   Responsive heart entwine.
Think not at bed-time of me,
   Nor on your pillow weep,

Nor dream that I am lonely,
  Or sinking in the deep.
Believe not I am lying
  In some damp prison cell,
Or on the cold ground dying;
  Dear mother, fare thee well!

Kind sister, keep up courage,
  There's hope and joy to come,
And peace again shall flourish,
  When battles have been won.
While on the mountain sleeping,
  I'll turn my thoughts to thee,
And fancy you are weeping,
  And mother, too, for me.
But try to ease her sorrow,
  And tell her I am well!
And hope for every morrow;
  Dear sister, fare thee well!

Dear brother, you are smaller,
  And younger far, than I ;
But time will make you taller,
  And fit to fight and die.
If I should never come back,
  And war continue still,
Take up my gun and knapsack,
  And fight for me who fell.
Let not a tyrant conquer
  Where our forefathers dwell,

H

Show slaves the free are stronger;
Dear brother, fare thee well!

I see the cloud of danger,
Brave England, round thy coast,
And rather than the stranger
Should humble thy proud boast,
My little all I give thee—
My heart, and hand, and life;
'Tis joyful thus to serve thee,
To die in freedom's strife.
Then wave the standard freely!
Let shouts of victory swell!
To conquer now I leave thee;
Dear England, fare thee well!

THE DANCE OF DEATH

At the Cavalry Action of Balaklava, 25th October, 1854.

COME boys, lead off the dance of death,
A dash and on we sally;
We left our homes to yield our breath,
So charge into this valley.
The Russians there, with sabres bare,
And pointed guns, are ready

To sweep us down, whose numbers are
  So few, to theirs so many.
But never mind their shots and knives,
  To die is but to die, O !
Our country kind demands our lives,
  To death's jaws fast we fly, O !

O handsome Death ! how nice you look,
  With cheeks all pale and bloody ;
Play up a tune, and let us foot
  Straight out of life that's ruddy.
These eyes we now can move about,
  As if they were our own things,
Are coin commanders must lay out
  To purchase ground for home-kings ;
Then take the coin and buy the land,
  Perchance you may not win it ;
And think of our devoted band,
  When we lie cold within it.

We light dragoons have silent been,
  While others have been fighting ;
Unsmeared with blood, we look too clean,
  And many mouths are chiding.
We stood impatient for the fray,
  But dare not move—they know that ;
Still nothing offered in our way
  But Russians thick and compact ;

But hark! we get an order, just
    To clear us from aspersions!
It sounds as if some madman's lust
    Would sport with Death's diversions!

"No time to spare! no time to spare!
    Recapture those Turk's guns, quick!
Your blood must buy the iron ware,
    Your horses hungry run sick!"
Then dance away to merry note,
    Dash through that scorching thunder!
We bound, we fly, as soon as spoke,
    And hearts are split in sunder!
Hot, raging, bleeding, down they fall,
    'Neath sword, and shot, and shell-fire!
Then Murder feasted at this ball,
    Beneath the glare of hell-fire!

And now the day may quick go by,
    The sun may set and night come;
There's blood enough to satisfy,
    But not a single gun won!
We might have saved so many lives,
    But dying was the fashion;
So we gave sport to Russian's knives,
    And danced to Death's red passion!
Now if you wish more blood to spill,
    Our veins are cold and empty;

No more commands can we fulfil,
But England's sons are plenty.

This "charge," a grievous rash mistake,
And fatal misadventure,
Was caused by one who shared the fate,
Whoever shares the censure.

NOTES OF THE NIGHTINGALE

At the Battle of Inkerman, 5th November, 1854.

UT on the carnage plain,
Cheering the bleeding slain,
She in a tender strain,
    Sings to the brave.
This bird of compassion,
Shuns high life and fashion,
Forsakes the rich bowers
Where peace and gay flowers
Would their true homage pay,
To the charms of her lay;
And in mercy she sings
To his soul, as it wings
Away from the dying
Lone warrior lying;
And she sings not in vain,
For she eases his pain,

And attends to his words
With a flock of trained birds,
Who respond to his moans
In benevolent tones
Which relax not till death
Seals the patriot's breath ;
When they part with their trust,
Who, again turned to dust,
      Wants but a grave.

On the war-aching world,
See her banner unfurled !
In meek opposition
To tyrant's ambition—
      Freely it floats.
In the wilds of the fight,
Through the day and the night,
She sings without ceasing,
With labours increasing—
      These are her notes :
Bring them in carefully,
Raise their heads tenderly,
Stanch their wounds cheerfully,
      Heroes of home.
The battle was frightful ;
May God help the rightful,
And pardon the spiteful,
      In times to come.

Wash off these clots of blood,
Filling their eyes like mud;
Bathe their pale temples fast,
Life may remain at last;
Who can tell whether yet
Danger has in them set?
These are the sons who went,
    Early to-day,
Forward with hearts content,
    Into the fray;
Not a murmur was heard—
No, not one grumbling word,
As they dashed through that rain,
Where, all smarting with pain,
They fought hard and struggled
Against numbers doubled;
That post was their honour—
    They held it fast;
And England's old banner
    Showed as it passed,
Its primitive net-work,
Torn in that red wet-work;
In hands cut and bleeding,
Whose lives were fast feeding
Death that had entered them,
Yet not prevented them;
Bore through the smoke and fire,
Victory's standard higher,
Shouting, undaunted still,

England is free!
She shall be monarch still,
    Queen of the sea!

Make them a bed of rest,
Now they have done their best;
    Glory's their own!
Bring them in carefully,
Raise their heads tenderly,
Stanch their wounds cheerfully,
    Heroes of home!

THE END.

UNWIN BROTHERS, PRINTERS, BUCKLERSBURY, E.C.

www.ingramcontent.com/pod-product-compliance
Lightning Source LLC
Chambersburg PA
CBHW022138020726
47496CB00008B/2448